PLAY ME

DRAGONS LOVE CURVES

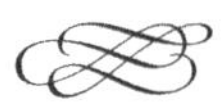

AIDY AWARD

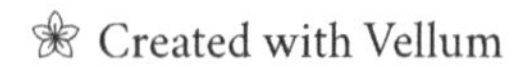
Created with Vellum

This book is dedicated to Dolly Parton for being a cool-ass human being. Not that she'll likely ever see this, but never the less, this book wouldn't be any good without her as an inspiration.

And to anyone who ever got the song 'Jolene' stuck in their head.
Because it sure as heck was stuck in mine the entire time I was writing this book.
Oops. I probably got it stuck in yours again now too.
Sorry, not sorry.

Love is game that two can play, and both win by losing their heart.

— EVA GABOR

AUTHOR'S NOTE

Lena's mom suffers from CPTSD stemming from the trauma in her past (namely the death of her husband) and agoraphobia. And to be honest, I put a lot of my own mental health struggles into that characters. The pandemic, which I not so fondly refer to as Coronapocalypse, has been hard on our collective mental health, and one of the fun things (read difficult things) that's come of it for me is that I HATE to leave my house now.

It's exhausting. The people out in the world are dumb. (They aren't, but my patience and willingness to give any fucks is very thin!) The big difference between me and Mrs. Walker is that I'm not afraid to go out, I just don't freaking want to.

But there's also the side of the story where Lena has to deal with her mother's mental illness. There were times in this story that I thought I may be too harshly portraying Lena's frustrations with her mother's mental health.

But that too is me in a metaphorical way. Lena's frustrations and feeling stuck taking care of her mother are my frustrations feeling stuck and trying to take care of my mental health battling anxiety, depression, and crazy weird symptoms of being neurodivergent. All which has been exacerbated by Coronapocalypse.

In the last few months, I've become more aware that some of my books might need trigger warnings. Which I never thought I would need to include, because I don't write dark romance - there will NEVER be any sexual assault or sexual violence against women in my stories, which in the past is what most trigger warnings were about.

But I've realized recently that because I write about curvy women, there are often moments of fatphobia in my books and that can be triggering for people. And because I also include struggles with mental health in my stories, that too might need a warning for readers who just aren't ready to deal with that.

So for the first time ever, I'm putting a trigger warning in the book so readers who want/need to check triggers before reading can.

NOT ALL WHO WANDER ARE LOST

Taika grumbled all the way across the Indian Ocean. He scowled at the beautiful mermaids he would have normally stopped and flirted with as he rounded the Cape of Good Hope and headed up the African coast. He snarled so hard at a school of tuna as he swam up the coast that they probably canceled class and closed up for the day.

"Hey there, Taika." A sparkly pink tailed Mami Wata mermaid waved to him and batted her long dark lashes at him. "Care for a swim?"

Quite a few Blue Dragon Warriors found their fated mates among the sweet and sassy African mermaids. He would have been perfectly happy to have found his here too. No luck.

It took all his mental energy not to growl at her and swish her away with his tail. It wasn't her fault he was in a shitty mood, and he hated being an asshole. *"Sorry, sweet girl. Off on Wyr business. No time to play."*

What a shame. Under any other circumstances, he would have stayed and done a whole lot more than playing. Her big boobs, soft, rounded belly, and big, dimpled butt was exactly his type. Or it used to be. Fuck, what was wrong with him?

He sped along at top speed to avoid running into anymore Mami Wata mermaids that lived in those waters. Any number of them would be ready to get their flirt on with him, and he couldn't care less. Normally, he'd use the North Atlantic Current to speed him across the ocean, but that was a busy route for water folk, mermaids, dragons, and more. Which meant interacting with them, and peopling was the last thing he wanted to do right now.

He headed for the open waters and used his power over the element to propel him just as fast as a current would have. That gave him the next few hours to let Moana's deep blue calm and quiet soothe him. He couldn't show up in his sour-ass mood. Second Wyvern's had to be open and approachable since they were often the one Wyr business was brought to first.

His mood wasn't likely to get any better when he hit the Eastern Seaboard of the United States. Not even if Ky had promised him that the supernatural community in Rogue would welcome him back with open arms. He was sure they were all perfectly nice, but New York was not

New Zealand, and that was the only place he wanted to be.

He'd had enough America for one lifetime. It wasn't the Americans he didn't like. He'd lusted over half a dozen local hens during the celebrations following the Dragon Warriors' defeat of the forces of Hell. He simply knew that what he was searching for wasn't anywhere near America. Not in Rogue, not in their big noisy cities, not in their quaint quiet towns.

His mate wasn't American.

She couldn't be.

He would have found her the last time he was here if she was. He was the Second Wyvern of the Blue Dragons, which meant he'd been chosen above all others for his prowess, his cunning, his fighting abilities, and that one special skill all Blue Dragon Warriors had—his ability to find anything.

He was the best.

Granny lost her favorite reading glasses? Taika could find them.

Little tyke lost his homework for school? Taika knew exactly where it was.

Missing car keys? Lost sunnies? Doggo gone walkabout? Taika was the one everyone called. He could find anything.

Except his one true mate.

So many Blue Dragon Warriors had found their mates and he was genuinely happy for them all. He'd stood up as witness or performed many a mating ceremony in the last year, giving lots of congratulations to one and all. There were still plenty of his brethren who hadn't found their mates either. So, it shouldn't bother him that he hadn't found his.

Granted, he was the last one of the dragons he knew well into his Prime who hadn't found a mate. As each one of his friends' soul shards lit up and they joined with the one woman or man in the world made for them and who they were made for, he got a little bit more worried that there was something wrong with him.

He had way more important things to do then represent the Blue Dragon Wyr in the shifter games.

Ky and Jada disagreed. He'd already gotten forty-seven messages asking when he would arrive from Ky and another twelve from Jada pretending to be Ky. He could tell the difference between his Wyvern's texts and his mate's because hers always included emojis. Usually food related ones. She had a thing for calling him a squirting potato.

He'd really hoped if he delayed his trip across the ocean long enough, some kind of Wyr emergency would come up to keep him in the Antipodes. But there hadn't been even a stubbed toe to keep him from going. Now he'd be the last to arrive in someplace called the Smoky Mountains in a landlocked area called Tennessee. Sure didn't sound like any place a Blue Dragon Warrior wanted to hang out. Certainly no place a mate to a water dragon would be either.

Best to just get this whole thing done and dusted so he

could go home or better yet, go exploring some tropical ocean and its islands filled with beautifully brown women and their lush, welcoming bodies. Just because he hadn't found his one true mate, didn't mean he couldn't have a little fun while looking for her.

Although, for the first time since he'd come of age and discovered the luscious pleasure to be found in a soft, warm, willing woman's body, he wasn't interested in any of them. Not in the least. There was a time when he'd be turned on by a dripping sink, and now, even porn couldn't get him off. And he'd tried. Often.

He'd walk around rock hard for days, and no matter how much he jerked off, he couldn't fucking come.

Which was probably half of the reason why he was so damn cranky these days. He really fucking needed to get laid. Which wasn't going to happen hanging out with all the other Wyverns, Seconds, and their mates. Maybe the shifter games would be good for him, because kicking everyone else's ass in each of the trials would help him burn off all this sexual energy he had but couldn't release to save his life.

He hit the coast near Rogue a few hours later. It was just a few days before the summer solstice, and that meant the beaches were overflowing with humans enjoying the sun and surf. He shooed away a few young sharks who'd come to investigate the splashes, and then shifted into his human form for the swim to shore.

Thank the Goddess the magic he used to shift from dragon to human included whatever he was already wearing. Since he lived most of his life on New Zealand's beaches anyway, that meant trunks, jandles, and his ever-present soul shard on a cord around his neck.

As he strode up onto the shore amongst the beachgoers, he let the water slide off his skin. There were far too many people here for his liking and they were all staring. Americans were so fucking weird.

What in the world was going on with these people? Had he left his horns unshifted? Or maybe his tail? He smoothed his hair, turned to check his backside just in case. It wasn't like him to make such a gaffe, but his mind was elsewhere. No tail or scales in sight.

"Whoa. Nice one, dude." A teenage boy heading toward the water lifted his hand for a high five. Must be his tattoo. His mark of the dragon was displayed loud and proud right across his chest.

Taika got his bearings and walked toward the town, but not three steps into his route, a group of young ladies on a beach blanket nearby burst into giggles. Then a woman pulled her son away, who was pointing and staring, and scowled at Taika. "This is a family friendly beach, young man. Control yourself or I'll report you to the lifeguards for lewd behavior."

What?

The woman narrowed her eyes, then dropped them pointedly to his mid-section, and then looked back up at him with one eyebrow raised and her lips pursed.

It wasn't as if he'd forgotten to put pants on or something. He glanced down and sighed. He was wearing his average, loose-fitting trunks. But even with plenty of room that would normally hide just about any sin, the front was tented like he had a fricking barracuda inside.

He didn't. That was just his cock. Making sure the whole damn world knew it was seeking out his mate.

Too bad he couldn't use it as a compass to point him to her. No, instead he was scaring off women and children with his giant hard on. Great. Just fucking great.

"Sorry, ma'am." He hurried away because it wasn't like there was actually much he could do. He didn't have a towel or anything to hide his not-so-little situation behind. Sweet Moana, what was wrong with him?

It wasn't like he could walk around town looking like a randy teenage perv. Okay, okay. Think of plastics in the ocean, acid rain, deserts, how long he had to wait for the new Aquaman movie to come out, and the fact that he still hadn't found his true mate.

Yeah, that last one did it. His cock went from a seek and destroy missile to cold shower shriveled just like that. Phew.

This was half of why he hated being on land. If he could, he'd spend every waking hour in the ocean. Now he was headed to a landlocked state called Tennessee and going up in the mountains to boot. Did they even have rivers or lakes up there? Who knew? Not him, because he'd avoided even thinking about this trip as long as he possibly could.

In fact, he'd be the last competitor to arrive. Which

was fine by him. The less time he had to spend away from the ocean, the better.

Taika followed his nose into town. He'd only been here the one time. But he knew to follow his nose when he picked up the scent of fresh baked pies to take him all the way to the shop that fronted for the Troika's speakeasy, The Sleepy Folk. This was where he'd catch his ride to the games.

"What can I get you?" A sweet and plump wahini, whose old-fashioned diner style dress read *Lila* just above her ample, right breast, gave him a sparkly-eyed smile from behind the counter. If he wasn't such a dumbass, he'd smile back and charm the pants off of her. Instead, he looked at the pies and ordered seven. It was a long swim after all.

The fruit-filled desserts were delish, but one of these days he'd have to insist Jada taught these wolf-shifters how to make a good old-fashioned steak and stout pie. Ooh, or even better, jellied eel and mash. He paid, looked around to make sure no one else was listening, and leaned in to speak quietly. "I'm here for a ride."

"Ru-duh." Her voice came out both offended and teasing. "Just because I smiled doesn't mean you can hit on me at my place of work."

"Uh." He grabbed his pile of pies and took a step back. Maybe this employee wasn't in on the paranormal nature of her employer, and the whole damn town for that matter.

Another woman popped out from the back with a tray

fresh out of the oven, glanced at her colleague, and did a double take at him. "Lila, you know dragons don't have a sense of humor. Don't tease them."

The cashier shrugged and winked at him. Well, half-winked, half scrunched up her cheek and had a sort of fit with her face. "Sorry, Key. I'm not good at flirting, I guess. Didn't mean to freak you out."

The new woman, whose uniform read *Kiana,* waved her away to take care of stocking the fresh pies and shook her head at him. "Sorry about that. She's kind of awkward around hot—"

Mid-sentence, Kiana's head tipped back, and her eyes went from human to a hauntingly eerie full-blown blue-gray, like she was an alien or something. Taika took a step back, but Kiana's hand shot out and grabbed his wrist. She opened her mouth and started belting some kind of twangy song about a woman called Jolene.

Fuck. Americans were so damn weird.

He tried to extricate himself from her death grip on his arm, but the more he tried, the louder she got. The chorus to the song had this Jolene name so many times over and over, he was definitely going to have the song stuck in his head. It was awful, too. Something about stealing someone's man.

Then just as quick as it started, the blue faded from Kiana's eyes, and she slumped against the counter. Taika grabbed her shoulders before she fell, and she looked up at him dazed. "Sorry, did I do it again?"

"Do what?" Scream out bad karaoke?

"Have a premonition." She stood back up straight, whatever affliction she had apparently over. She straightened her uniform and wiped away invisible crumbs. "Well, whatever I said to you, I can't tell you what it means. I don't even know what I said. That's just sort of how it works. Sorry."

A premonition? About someone named Jolene who steals men?

Great.

HOT SAUCED AND BOTHERED

Just one more bar-stomping song and Lena would have her rent money, and well before the first of the month. The rowdy bunch of cowboys that came in a half hour before closing and ordered pretty much three of every meat on the menu were gonna leave her the biggest ass tip she could get out of them. Even if that meant she had to shake her big ass for them.

Because if she had rent money by the end of tonight, that meant everything else she earned this week could go toward her maybe someday fund.

Maybe someday she could leave Walker Valley for good instead of only for her crazy vacations. Not that her mama would be pleased if she stayed gone that long.

Maybe someday she'd never have to come back.

Maybe someday.

She jumped up on the bar counter and snagged the

microphone. It totally wasn't her turn to sing, but Billy's version of some depressing Johnny Cash song wasn't going to get the dollar bills. He gave her a glare but leaned back onto the nearest barstool and gave that damn toothpick he was always chewing on a couple of flips with his lips.

He thought he was sexy when he did that. Lena thought he looked like a duck. There were promises of retribution in that toothpick flip. Fine. She knew how to share the spotlight and a duet always got the room honky tonkin' and the tips flowing. "Come up and sing *Islands in the Stream* with me."

Flip. "I ain't no boring ass Kenny Rogers."

"Maybe not, but the sorority girls on their summer vacay over at table four don't know the difference. It'll get them all giggly and hot and bothered. You know it will." Appealing to his libido was the surest way to get him to do her this favor.

Billy glanced over to the table that belonged to Dixie Sue, who impersonated Minnie Pearl. But Dix was about four-thousand months preggo and would be grateful if Billy took over closing the table out as long as he split the tips with her. Lena would make sure he did. Her cousin needed every last penny and dime to help welcome a new member of the fam into the valley.

"Fine. But you owe me, Neener Leener."

She barely kept herself from rolling her eyes. Billy was convinced he was so fucking clever with his nicknames for everyone. Someday, when she didn't need this seasonal job, she'd tell him how bad he sucked at those, and singing, and for that matter, serving, performing, and impersonating anyone but a douchepotato. If his mama didn't own the Grand Ole Eatery, he'd have to sell used cars with his daddy over in Gatlinburg.

Instead of slapping him upside the head like she wanted to, Lena reached out her hand, and he hopped up on the bar with her. He snagged the microphone out of her hand and sauntered down the wooden countertop. "Anybody out there lonesome tonight?"

Bless his heart. He was fixin' to do an Elvis song without her. Nuh-uh, no way. Lena grabbed the second microphone, winked at the boys at her table and then gave Billy the thumbs down and a big, loud raspberry. "Pthth. We don't want no lonesome nights in here, do we fellas?"

The room gave her exactly the response she was hoping for. Boos and hoots and hollers burst out, jeering Billy's show stealing tactics. Someone who didn't know any better yelled out, "Do Jolene."

Nope. Never gonna happen. Lena ignored them and tapped the karaoke machine that served as their entertainment hub. The opening chords of the duet started up. A good half the crowd clapped when they recognized the song and that's all she needed to get them going. "That's right. Let's give these hard-working, hard-playin' folks a rootin' tootin' love song."

Tourist season didn't officially kick off until tomorrow with the annual Rhubarb Festival, so most of the people in here tonight were Walker Valley locals. That was fine by her. Local tips were just as good as tourist ones.

Billy gave her a stink-eye, but he started singing right on cue. Even he wasn't dumb enough to pitch a fit in front of a crowd.

Lena would pull out her best acting skills to make the whole room believe she had the hots for Billy if it got them riled up. She batted her eyelashes at him, smiled nice and big, and when it came time for the chorus, she turned to her tables and raised her arms to get them to join in. Within moments they had the whole room waving their arms in the air, singing about being lovers to each other, wah-uh.

When the song ended, they got the cheers they were looking for, and with closing time not far off, those wallets would be nice and open. Lena gave Billy a little pat on the cheek because she certainly wasn't going to kiss him and hopped down off the bar. She grabbed the closest pitcher of tea to refill her diners' glasses and headed back to her section of the dining room.

There were big smiles all around, and that always meant generous tips. She gave her good-luck charm necklace a quick kiss to thank the universe and mentally planned her next trip. Maybe she'd head back down to Mexico where her money would last the longest. But maybe she'd have enough this time to go all the way down to the tip of South America.

But as she approached the nearest table, the faces

went from happy, happy, joy, joy, to wide-eyed surprise. One guy's jaw fell open wide enough to let flies in. What? Did her shirt pop open? Were her boobs hanging out for all to see her functional, not so cute bra?

She patted her chest and glanced down. Nope. She turned, thinking maybe her skirt was caught up and her butt was hanging out or something. That's when she saw the tall, tanned, far-too-sexy for-his-own-good stranger standing in the doorway.

But instead of greeting him, she nearly missed tripping over Billy, and ran smack dab into Dixie coming through with a full tray of hot chicken sandwiches and slices of rhubarb pie. Every single one of which landed directly up and down her front, from her neck to her knees. She was going to smell like hot sauce and rhubarb for a damn week.

The room yipped and cheered as if the Vols had scored the game winning touchdown. She swiped the pie off real quick, since she was allergic to rhubarb. Phew, no hives. Well, maybe she'd get some sympathy tips out of it.

The handsome stranger took a step back. His eyes were watering so bad, tears were streaming down his face, and he started sneezing something awful. It didn't take him long to hightail it toward the restroom.

"Shoot, sorry Lena. You better hurry to the back and strip out of that mess before it gets in your hair. I'll get your tables for a minute since I gotta russle up more hot chickens and slices anyway." Dixie bent to start picking up the mess and grunted and groaned like a barn door in a windstorm.

"No, no. I've already got it all over me. I'll get this mess. You refill those teas for me."

"Thanks, sweetie. You're the best." Dixie carefully handed over the now empty tray and took the somehow unspilled pitcher of tea.

After a long sigh, which also pushed the scent of sweet pie filling and spicy chicken out of her nose, Lena bent to her work. Some jackasses behind her whistled a dreaded catcall. No women she knew liked that sound. Why any man thought whistling like that was a compliment and not just creepy was beyond her.

Heat and hive-like tingles rushed right up Lena's neck and cheeks. She adjusted her stance to a squat, so her rear end wasn't sticking straight up for all to see or whistle at and ignored the creep. Her past experience with this kind of situation was that the next comment was going straight into some kind of obnoxious fatphobia.

Ninety percent of the time, she really liked who she was and didn't give a hoot or a holler what some scumbag thought about the way she looked. But she was feeling a bit rattled and more vulnerable than normal. Being doused in hot chicken sauce and sugary rhubarb syrup would do that to a girl.

"Now, Dolly, you were shaking your ass for us earlier, don't quit now just because you're all hot and bothered." Shit on a shingle, she knew that voice. Once a high school tormentor, always one. Some people never grew up or moved on.

Eyeroll. If she didn't stop this trainwreck in its tracks, she'd be sorry later. She turned just her head toward him, to tell him off and still get her work done. "Look—"

Tormentor had gone quiet and now she could see why. Tall, dark, and stranger was back and holding the jackass up in the air by his collar. "That is a pretty sus way to speak to any sheila. I suggest you apologize before I give you a hiding."

Ooh, now that was one sexy accent. This stranger definitely wasn't home grown Appalachian. Australia maybe? Wherever it was, she wanted to go.

Jackass kicked his feet and squeaked out something, but it wasn't any kind of apology. More like a litany of unrecognizable epitaphs. Dude was legit speaking in tongues. If she didn't intervene, this thunder from down under might actually choke him out.

Decisions, decisions.

Handsome stranger didn't back down for a second, not even when the rest of the table got up like they were gonna fight him. He gave them a look that felt more like a six-foot bear, or a lion, or something bigger and scarier, telling some whiner babies to back off. Wait, did he actually growl? "Quit packing a sad there bro and apologize to the lady."

Bully boy squealed worse than a stuck pig, and her handsome foreign stranger gave him a shake. "Did that sound like an apology to anyone else?"

Okay, she could get on board with this. Especially that accent. Oh, wait, no, no, the bully thing was still happening. Not a good time to offer to buy her yummy stranger a drink.

Sure, sure violence was never the answer and all that. Except some bullies didn't speak any other language. She might not need a man to protect her, but she wasn't going to say no to this brand of support. Maybe if someone had stood up to this bully when they were teenagers, he might have learned his lesson back then.

Now was as good a time as any.

So instead of telling the handsome stranger to put her customer down, she folded her arms across her sauce-covered blouse and tapped her foot. "Didn't sound like one to me."

If she wasn't the main reason Tuesday, Thursday, and Saturday nights, and Sunday brunch were packed, she might be worried she'd lose her job over this. But the Whitecap family that owned the diner liked bringing home the bacon just as much as she did. They might give her a stern warning, but they wouldn't let her go.

Jackass squeaked, probably from getting his windpipe crushed little by little. He was looking a bit blue in the face. Or... wait, the stranger had a blue glow coming from some kind of a pendant he wore. He looked down at his chest, balked, and dropped his prey right in the middle of the table.

He looked around the room, frantic like. Was the necklace an alarm of some kind? It wasn't as if he'd fallen and couldn't get up. Lena would bet that night's tips he could get it up just fine. No, he wasn't worried or scared. That was some kind of delighted surprise on his face.

What in the world did he think he was going to discover in the middle of nowhere Tennessee at a mediocre diner right before closing time? She full-well knew there was nothing worth finding round these parts.

Jackass squirmed and made like he was going to get up and start a fight, but the stranger put one huge hand over his face and shoved him back down. Then he sniffed the air, once again reminding her of some kind of alpha animal on the hunt.

He swiveled his head her way, took a long sniff and boom, that hot sauce hit his olfactory senses again and he sneezed like a volcano going off. His eyes watered and puffed up and his nose went as snotty as a four-year-old.

"I'd offer you a napkin, but I think it's me you're having an allergic reaction to." She pointed him toward the restrooms off to the right, but he sneezed again and backed away. Before she could tell him to go wash up or ask if she needed to get out the epi-pen from the first aid kit, he bolted out the front door and into the dark without another word.

"I sure hope he's okay," Dixie Sue said from behind the counter.

"He can fuck off and die in the woods for all I care." Billy, who'd been nowhere to be found during the whole dang incident, finally showed up and guided Lena's harasser and friends into their booth. Once a Whitecap always a Whitecap. "Your meals are on the house of course."

Cripes. Wasn't like they were gonna tip her and Dixie Sue anyway. She sure wished the out-of-town hottie had stuck around though. She would have bought him a drink or something to say thank you very much. Although, if she was honest, she could think of some other ways to show her gratitude that involved a whole lot less clothes.

Whoa. Where did that thought come from? On principle, she didn't do casual sex. If she was getting naked with someone it was either because they were chunky dunkin'—she had too much junk in her trunk to call it skinny dippin'—or because they were in a deeply committed relationship.

She didn't ever want anyone to claim she lived up to her namesake.

With her backside facing in the opposite direction this time, Lena finished cleaning up the mess of chicken and buns, tossing them all on a serving tray and popping it behind the bar to take care of later. Dixie Sue brought out the free replacement sandwiches and sides in to-go containers. Thank goodness it was almost closing time.

Lena slipped into the back and grabbed one of the diner's t-shirts from the merchandise stack and slipped into the break room to get out of her ruined uniform. She peeled out of the top as best she could, but that sauce was freaking everywhere. Even in her hair or rather her wig.

Now that she was out of the goopy shirt, she felt overly bare. Oh shoot. Her necklace was missing. It had to have fallen in the crash. There hadn't been a day since she was knee-high to a grasshopper that she wasn't wearing that charm. It was her only connection to her daddy.

There wasn't really enough time to get a proper clean-up, not if she didn't want Billy closing out her tabs and stealing her tips. She used some make-up wipes to get most of the remaining mess off, and then yanked the slightly too tight t-shirt on over her head. Nothing ever fit properly over her boobs. They were such a pain in the chest, and back. She popped back out to look for her necklace and close out her tabs.

She looked around the floor and table but didn't see her necklace anywhere. Crudmuffins. It would have to wait another few minutes. She closed out the rest of the tabs, got her customers taken care of and out the door with nary a grumble, all the while keeping her eye out for the sparkle from the gold chain or the little charm.

The rest of her tables had definitely taken sympathy on her, or just enjoyed the shenanigans of the night, and all tipped her real good. Rent was definitely covered. But still no necklace.

Billy bolted the second his drawer was counted out, like he had somewhere better to be. He didn't even bother to say goodbye. Dixie Sue looked slap worn out. "Go on now, Dix, I can lock up. Check that my mama turned her lights out and locked her door for me, will ya?"

Closing up here gave her more time to search for her missing piece of jewelry, and she didn't have to swing by her mother's house if her cousin, who lived next door, would do it for her.

"I ain't gonna argue with you. Don't worry about your mama." Dix grabbed her purse and headed out the front door where her cinnamon roll of a husband had the engine running waiting on her.

The diner's kitchen crew was fast as lightning on their closing checklist and had the dishes done, the trash taken out, and were hanging up their aprons before Lena remembered the tray of nasty floor chicken. "Please, oh please, let my necklace be on that tray."

She grabbed it and pushed the mess around, carefully feeling for her necklace before throwing each squishy piece into the trash. Under the very last orange bun, she finally spotted the gold chain shining through the sauce. "Yes. Thank you, sweet baby Jesus."

Lena snagged the chain and charm out of the orange mess and almost dropped it again. It buzzed in her fingers like an angry bumblebee. No, that wasn't quite right. More like a high-speed, low drag vibrator. In fact... either she was going crazy, or she could feel that humming everywhere from her fingers to her spine and down, down, down between her legs.

It wasn't like the hot chicken sauce turned her on. What in the Sam Hill had her so hot and bothered?

Sexy strangers. That's what.

SWEET AS

Taika pulled a branch out from under his knees that had been poking him for the past half an hour. He'd hunkered down into the copse of bushes at the edge of the parking lot, well hidden from the eyes of the humans. They couldn't see him, but he watched them get into their ridiculously large American cars and trucks and drive away. Did he feel like a weird stalker? Yes. Was he going to sit here and watch each and every person leave this diner and sniff them? Also yes.

Shit. Was he a stalker?

Once again. Yes.

He would continue his psycho impersonation, because his fucking soul shard had lit up like a love beacon. His fated mate was nearby. But where? Somehow while all of his friends had found mates, not a one of them had ever said exactly how they knew she was the one. He assumed he'd just know. But he hadn't.

He could find anything in the whole goddamn world except his own one true love, even when his soul shard said she was right the fuck in front of him. He was cursed. That had to be it. Other Dragon Warriors had been cursed in extra special ways, so that was the most logical explanation.

Either that, or he wasn't actually destined to have a fated mate to love and cherish, and his soul shard lighting up was just some kind of prank the Universe was playing on him. Because as he sat there and weirdo sniffed and scented all the humans coming out of the diner, none were his mate.

The lights went out and the last three people made their way out the doors and to their cars. Two men who mostly smelled of soap, and the waitress with the luscious ass. He wasn't opposed to his mate being male, but he felt little to nothing when he checked the men out as they got into their cars, and soap wasn't exactly on his list of aphrodisiacs. So, no to either of them.

That left the woman and just thinking about her had his eyes watering again. He already knew she wasn't the one. Not that he couldn't imagine wrapping his hands around her thick thighs and diving in... shit, just the thought had the roof of his mouth burning. He backed away further into the brush and trees just so he wouldn't reveal his presence with another bout of sneezes.

She hummed a catchy little tune, and the wind rustled through the leaves. The scattered clouds overhead parted and moonlight shined down on her, lighting her way to her car. Taika's stomach growled and her head snapped to look in his direction.

He had gone in the diner to get something to eat and had been forced to quite literally flee before he'd even been able to order. Probably a good thing if what they served was slathered in that repulsive hot sauce. That's what he got for eating nothing but fruit pies instead of hunting before he came to this landlocked town. They probably didn't even have any fish or seafood on the menu.

With a hand over his belly, he kept very still. Unlikely that she'd spot him anyway. He might not be able to find his mate, but he could find a good hiding spot.

She gave a shake of her head and got into her car. For a minute, Taika considered following her into the busier part of town just to see what kind of place it was. Even if he couldn't get whoever he or she was all the way to Aotearoa, he'd have to work hard to convince her that beach living was better than these mountains. He already missed the smell of the salt in the air.

Anything was better than that hot sauce.

He watched the taillights of her car until they were out of sight and then went back to circle the diner just in case there was some clue to who his mate might be. The light from his soul shard dimmed a bit and he sighed. Once it was lit from within, the glow would never fade completely, but it was seeming to indicate that he'd lost the trail.

Dammit. Fine. It was well past time that he checked in

with Ky to let him know he's arrived. Taika opened his mind to speak with his king, the Wyvern of the Blue Dragons. He should be close enough to make the mental connection.

"Hey, Douchepotato."

That voice popped into his head and was there and gone faster than he could identify the Dragon Warrior. It had been so fleeting and quiet that he wasn't even sure it had been mindspeak and not someone else nearby. "Hello?"

Taika pushed his senses out, letting his dragon rise up so he could push his eyes, ears, and nose beyond what his weaker human form could perceive. All he found was a whole lot of wildlife he was completely unfamiliar with. Weird.

Great. Now he was hallucinating? *"Ky Puru, I am nearby."*

No response from his Wyvern. Huh.

The voice poked at him again. *"She was right in front of you."*

He'd never heard any other dragons in his head outside of his Wyr, and he knew every single one of them. He shouldn't be able to mindspeak with anyone else. Could that hot sauce be causing him to hallucinate?

"You could be giving her all the orgasms she desires right now, but no. You had to go and be an absolute potato."

Alright, enough was enough. *"Who you calling potato, coward? Show yourself and fight like a dragon."*

Taika shifted into his dragon form and pulled on the

power he had over his element. He might not be anywhere near the ocean, but there was plenty of water to be found at the base of these gentle mountains. A pipe burst on the side of the diner, and the leaves on the trees and ground shook as the air filled with thousands of sparkling beads of water waiting for their orders.

If he had a target, he could freeze those droplets hard and direct them as projectiles, shooting his opponent down. He swished his tail and grabbed a hold of the stream pouring from the pipe. He swirled it around, creating a whip that could cut through flesh.

"Taika?" Jada appeared in the light of the diner's sign. Oh fuck. Was this unknown entity after his Wyvern's mate? He would defend her with his life if need be, but she just tipped her head to one side and then the other looking at him like he was some kind of bizarre sea creature. "What in the world are you doing? You're a bit late for practice. Besides the shifter gauntlet isn't until the last trial."

"Taika Puru, stand down and shift." Ky's alpha voice rang through Taika's ears, boring into his brain, all the way to his soul. He could do nothing but obey that order.

He pushed his dragon back down and let the shimmer of magic all Dragon Warriors were gifted shift him back to his human form. His mind felt filled with Jell-O and he shook it, trying to get back to himself. "Ky, my apologies. I could swear there was someone else here, but I can't seem to remember who or what."

Jada and Ky exchanged a look that had Taika's chest

going tight. What did they know that he didn't? As Second, he should be made aware of any danger, especially to his Wyvern and his mate.

Before he could ask, Jada pointed to his chest. "Sweet sugar, Taika, your soul shard is glowing. That explains it."

"Explains what?"

Ky grinned and gave Taika a slap on the shoulder. "Sweet as, bro. Who woulda thought you'd find a mate out in the wops? Where is she?"

Taika blinked. "I have no idea what's going on right now."

Ky and Jada exchanged a knowing look and Ky laughed. "A lot of dragons and mates have a bit of missing time, or strange events happen to them around the time they find their mate. The going theory among the Wyverns is that it's the First Dragon and the White Witch hurrying us along. Good on ya. So where is your new missus?"

The First Dragon? No, that couldn't be right. He had the distinct impression he'd been talking to someone around his own age and who was a bit of a dick. "Nah, I'm having a mare today. I haven't found him or her. I think my soul shard is munted or something."

He waited a good long minute for Ky to say something like that happened all the time. He knew good and well it didn't. "Let's get you up the mountain. Then we'll talk to the other Wyverns about that and get you good as gold."

Bloody hell. He already felt like a potato, he didn't need every dragon he respected to know he and his soul were broken. "Ta, but I'll just pop back down to this small town and do some searching between the trials. I got this."

Ky gave him a nod, but Taika did not like the look in Jada's eyes. She was cooking up something and it wasn't her world-famous donuts. He should definitely be worried.

He and Ky shut off the water and quickly fixed the water line and then they shifted back into their dragon forms. Ky tucked Jada into his talons, and they flew up the mountain together as low to the tree line as possible so as not to be spotted. A soft current, that had the Gold Dragons' name all over it, guided them to a clearing in the trees.

At first Taika couldn't quite focus on the trees and grassy field and he thought maybe his bout with the unknown entity from earlier had affected him more than he realized. But Ky sent out a mental call and the fuzziness faded away.

Ah, someone had bespelled the area with some wards to obscure the gathering and playing field from the prying eyes of humankind. Smart. They circled and landed at one end of the clearing where most of the Dragon Warriors and their mates were gathered.

Ky placed Jada gently on the ground before they shifted back to their human forms. She hit the ground running and headed straight for the other Wyvern mates. Seconds later, there were squeals and all eyes turned to him.

Taika took three steps back. "Fuck. You gotta hide me, bro."

Ky chuckled. "You're in for it now. Have fun with that."

"Traitor."

The whole group of women hurried over and surrounded him. There was no escaping now.

He held still as Ciara examined the bone carving pendant that contained his soul shard. He supposed he could use her advice, since she was the first mate to break Ereshkigal's curse and find her mate, the Green Dragon Wyvern. She was also a white witch who had power over four elements. "Ooh, Jada, you're right. Mate alert for sure. It's definitely glowing."

Taika was only kidding himself that her supernatural powers would help him. They all knew she loved to get all up in everyone else's relationships mostly so she could plan mating ceremonies and weddings.

Jada clapped. "I know, right? What kind of mate do you think she is?"

"She's some kind of pretty powerful supernatural being if she's able to hide from him." Fallyn stroked her chin and nodded sagely.

Wait, what? "Who said anything about hiding?"

Did the alpha of all alpha's mate know something he didn't? All this speculation was making his skin itchy. He was more of a doing kind of dragon than sitting around and talking or speculating.

"But why would she hide from this hunka-hunk of

burning love?" Yvaine danced around as if she couldn't contain her own excitement. "If I didn't have Jett to keep me so very thoroughly satisfied, I'd totally go for a tatted-up hottie like Taika."

"Yvaine." Azy sighed. "We do not need to hear any more about your sex life today or tomorrow, or pretty much ever."

Yvaine froze in front of Azy and stuck out her bottom lip. "But I haven't even told you about—"

Azy's eyes went wide, and she quickly turned away. "Fallyn, you don't happen to hear Taika's mate, do you?"

"Nope. The only voice up here now is mine or Match's." Fallyn tapped her temple.

"Where exactly were you when your soul shard lit up, Taika?" Ciara asked.

Oh, great, so he was going to get to be involved in finding his own mate. That was fun. "I—"

"We ran into him at that cute diner at the bottom of the hill. You know, the one where they impersonate old country and western stars." Jada pointed toward the town as if they could all see it. "I was hoping to get some stuff to make breakfast before they closed, but we were too late."

Ciara rubbed her hands together like a legit villain plotting his demise. "Then we're going back there first thing in the morning. We must help our good Second Wyvern here find his mate."

Taika rolled his eyes. He wasn't going to get out of this. Might as well go along with it. His own finder skills were clearly broken. Plus, he'd been this close to his mate and missed him or her all together. So, he could use the help.

Jakob joined them and tugged Ciara into his arms. "*Miláčku,* the opening ceremonies of the shifter games are in the morning. Then the trials. It might have to wait."

"Love waits for no games."

If fate was playing a game with him trying to make him play some kind of twisted version of find the mate, this was one trial he was going to win.

HERE I COME AGAIN

Lena's phone rang for the third time in a row, so she threw her pillow at it. She was so not a morning person and most everyone in her life knew better than to call before nine in the morning. She was the epitome of the roll out of bed and stumble to the kitchen to pour herself a cup of ambition type of gal.

There was only one person who didn't care what time it was. Lena slid her phone out from under the pillow. "Hello, mama."

"You ain't going to the rhubarb festival today, are you?" Not hello, not how are you, not even good morning.

Lena had gone to the one and only interesting thing this town ever had since she'd been a teenager. And even then, it was just the one time. "No, Mama. I have to work."

"Good. Don't let me hear you snuck over there either."

If anyone sounded like a parody of an overprotective mother telling a wild child off, it was Lena's one and only parent.

"No, ma'am." Her mama might not still be able to tan her hide like she had back then, but her verbal lashes were just as painful.

"Good. Now quit being a laze-about and run and pick up my pills for me." Her tone changed from finger-wagging to woe is me. "I don't feel right today."

Mama never felt right. Next, she'd say this was probably her last year on Earth and get all sniffly. She was always sure this was her last summer, or she wasn't going to make it to next Christmas. She'd been dying for twenty years. And not a soul could blame her. Broken hearts were the worst kind of non-healing wounds.

Another call beeped in, and Lena hadn't ever been so grateful to see the diner on her caller ID. "I'm getting another call from work. I'll have the pharmacy bring your pills over. Gotta go."

She switched over to the other call before her mother could complain that she didn't care about her. "Hello?"

"Lena, can you come in early? We are frickin' slammed this morning." Lena could barely hear Mrs. Whitecap, the diner's owner over all the background noise. "Some kind of tourist group come in for the rhubarb festival. I've never seen so many hot men in my life."

Must be why her handsome bully buster was here too. She wouldn't mind getting to buy him some breakfast. Or better yet, make him breakfast after a long night of—

Geez Louise. He had gotten under her skin something fierce. Maybe it was better if she didn't see him again, because she might do something dumb like offer to have his children. They would be such cute babies too.

Another shift meant more money for the someday jar. "I'll be there as soon as I can."

Yeah, because she wasn't hoping to see that guy again or anything. No, nope. She'd do the dreaded clopening just for the money. Yep.

Ack. Okay, that was it. She was taking a cold shower this morning.

After that way too refreshing chilly water, she searched for something to wear. Her regular outfit was still soaking in the kitchen sink. It might take a month to get those stains out. She finally found an old western style cowgirl shirt, and a red-checked skirt that had seen better days.

Lena grabbed her necklace out of the cleaning solution she left it to sit in overnight and slipped it around her neck. The double-twisted infinity charm settled right over her heart and having it back on made all the difference in the world. She could breathe again. Although, it still had that slight buzz to it.

She didn't hate it, but she was gonna need another cold shower. Later. A dash to her car, a zip through town, and she was turning off the road and into the dirt parking lot.

She expected to see it packed with cars or tour buses or something, and it wasn't any fuller than a normal rhubarb festival morning. But the second she pulled open the door to go inside, the cacophony of a full house hit her smack dab in the face.

Not only were the townies packed in for the diner's once a year rhubarb pancakes, the booths were double packed with visitors. Where in the world did all these people come from and how were they going to get back there without cars?

The most beautiful round woman, dressed all in white, rushed by with a tray fully loaded up with stacks of pancakes and biscuits and gravy. "Hey doll, can you take table fourteen for me? They've been waiting a bit. Thanks."

For a full six or seven blinks, Lena stood there staring at the backside of the woman in white sashaying away to serve her table. So many questions and absolutely no time to ask. But seriously, who was that, what country and western or blue grass star was she supposed to be, and who wore all white to serve food in a busy diner? She'd have to find out after this insane rush.

Maybe she was Dixie Sue's replacement, because she wasn't anywhere to be seen. Surely her hubby would have called if they'd had the baby.

Lena tossed her bag behind the bar, grabbed menus, a tray of coffee mugs, and a fresh pot that had just finished brewing, and headed over to her table. Looked like a girls' weekend gone good with their fancy clothes, expensive haircuts, and stunning looks. They were dressed in the colors of the rainbow, except for one of the two blondes dressed in a shimmering black romper with a unicorn farting a rainbow on the front. How was it that every single woman in this group was so attractive? Were they some kind of plus-size models or something?

Then, tucked into the corner of the booth was the last person she expected to see. Or rather the one she'd hoped to.

Handsome, foreign stranger.

Well, dag nabbit. Either he was quite the ladies' man, getting himself a whole durn harem or he was someone's GBF. Either way, meant hands off for her. Sad.

Lena's necklace went wackadoodle against her skin and a sudden memory slammed into her. She'd had a full-on sex dream about that guy last night. His tongue and his yummy foreign accent had her seeing stars all night long. How. Freaking. Embarrassing.

Ahem. Hopefully he wouldn't notice how the red flush was creeping up her chest and cheeks. Still had to do her job after all. "Hello there, folks, sorry for the wait, we're a bit busier this morning than usual. What can I get you started with? Coffees all around?"

Before any of them answered her, the woman in green turned to handsome stranger and asked, "Ooh, Taika, you're umm, glowing. Is this her?"

Taika. She liked that name. It made her think dirty thoughts. That flush she was trying to hide tingled right up under her chin and had her ears tickling. He must have already told them about the incident last night. Gah.

Why couldn't she have gotten any other tables than this one?

Lena gave him a smile that she didn't mean as flirty, but simply friendly, even if that wasn't what she was feeling on the inside. She needed to just take their order and get a move on. "Hey there, nice to see you again. Your breakfast is on me as thanks for last night, although not literally this time if I can help it."

Wait. Did that just sound like the two of them had hooked up and she was offering to buy him breakfast because he'd given her a dozen and half orgasms? Yes. Yes, it had. It took a whole lot of willpower for Lena to not simply turn around and go hide in the kitchen.

Taika didn't seem to notice. Instead of hello, he sneezed and his eyes set to watering. Again. He shook his head and grabbed a napkin to blow his nose. "No. We met last night. It's not her. I think I'm actually allergic to her."

He sneezed about twelve more times.

"Okay, holy guacamole, Taika. You don't have to have a fit just because this pretty lady isn't your soul mate. I didn't even know dra—people in our family could have allergies." The woman with the unicorn romper said, and then slapped her hand over her mouth like she'd said something unspeakable. Everyone else rolled their eyes at her, but each of them also gave Lena a sort of surreptitious glance too.

Must be some kind of inside thing she wasn't privy to. Whatever. She needed to get the order and quit screwing around. She'd never dawdled so long at a table in her life.

"Okay, so no hot sauce for your table. That's okay, we've got plenty of options on the breakfast menu that are sweet and creamy, if you catch my drift."

She'd looked right at tantalizing Taika when she said creamy. Oh gawd. Her flirter had just revved right up and sped out of her mouth without her even trying. If he was gay, it wouldn't matter anyway. Then she went and gave him a wink. What in the tarnation did she do that for? It was like her hormones had taken over and decided she was a teenager.

He tipped his head to the side and gave her a cute, smirky smile like he thought her awkwardness was adorable. Sigh. Might as well just keep going as if that's how she treated all customers. "I'm guessing you're all here for the rhubarb pancakes since the festival starts today, but maybe you need a round of Just Call Me Angel of the Morning Bloody Marys. And if you don't want something sweet, you can't go wrong with the Mamas Don't Let Your Babies Grow Up To Be Biscuits and Gravy."

Now she was blathering. She never got this flustered. She'd been stuck in Walker Valley for too long if one handsome man had her turning into an awk-weird flirty waitress. And summer had only just started. She had the rest of the season before she could high tail it out of town again for a while. That was if her mama didn't pitch a big fit.

The woman in sunglasses pointed to her menu. "Did you say rhubarb pancakes? Uh-oh. Uh, family allergy."

She got up on her knees and patted the shoulder of the guy in the booth right behind them. "Sweetheart, let everyone know to avoid the pancake special. They're rhubarb."

"Bugger. Don't want anyone carking it. Thanks, *aroha.*" Her sweetheart had the same yummy accent as Taika and turned to the other men at his table, said something about rhubarb to them and they all got this sort of blank look on their faces.

Huh. Hadn't unicorn girl said they didn't have allergies? "I take it you're not here for the rhubarb festival, then. Headed over to Dollywood? Where are you folks in from?" Great. Now she was making chit chat. If she was going to do that, she might as well get the downlow on who this dreamy Taika guy was.

Taika tore up the napkin and stuffed two bits right up his nose. How was that actually cute? Like... so adorable. He motioned around the room to all the other tourists. "We're from all over. I'm a Kiwi, but most are from Europe."

Wow. She'd dreamed of visiting far off places but had only ever been to Mexico and Canada. Which was a whole lot more than the average Walker-Vallian had ever been. But Europe and the Antipodes? She could hardly imagine it. "What are you doing here?"

And can you stay a while... in my bed? Jeepers creepers. There was seriously something wrong with her today.

"Everybody's got to eat, so here we are at your, umm,

fun establishment." Taika grinned at Lena, and she forgot what he'd said. Hell, she forgot her own name. Then he sneezed again, and the tissues went flying out of his nose.

The ladies at the table looked from Taika to her and back again. Yeah, okay, she was being too friendly and only paying attention to him. Time to get their orders and quit flirting with the guy who wasn't even interested in her.

"We'd better get you folks fed so your yummy friend can get himself some Benadryl." Crap on a cracker, she'd just called him yummy. Sigh. "What'll ya have?"

Taika took a deep breath like he was going to sneeze again but got himself under control and asked. "Did you say something about biscuits with gravy on them? You're sure that's a good combo? Sounds pretty weird."

"Oh, yeah." Lena'd had this discussion once on a train through the Canadian Rockies last year with a nice young lady from England. "You're thinking cookies with brown sauce on them. That would be weird. Think light and fluffy scones with a peppery cream sauce and breakfast sausage. I promise it's good."

He made a sort of thinking face but with a smirky smile. "Okay. I'll try it."

Lena wrote down the order and then indicated to the next girl who was hmm-ing and haw-ing over her choices. "How about the Coal Miner's Daughter's Donuts?"

Sunglasses girl clapped her hands. "Yes. I didn't even see that. Sold."

"Me too," unicorn girl said.

"These are the worst menu item names I think I've ever seen." The woman wearing a gold silky shirt that really popped against her brown skin, snorted, and shook her head. "I'll have the Redneck Woman Shrimp and Grits. Fallyn, you want to share a Harper Valley P.T. Apple Fritter with me?"

Wait until they got a load of the entertainment.

The woman with the fiery red hair nodded and studied the menu some more. "Yes, please, and then I will also have one of my own. Any chance you can make that *en flambé*?"

Lena laughed and shook her head. "Umm, I don't think so. How about I just warm it up for you."

"Yeah. That's fine. Just make it really hot. And keep the hottest coffee you've got coming too, please. I didn't know this place would be so cold."

"I'll have the donuts too, please. And let me ask you something else," Ciara said. "You were working last night, right? Did you see anyone, let's say, umm, unusually attracted to our friend Taika, here?"

"Ciara." Taika growled her name, saying with that one word that she'd gone too far. They were clearly pretty good friends.

She wished he'd say her name like that.

"What?" Ciara said all innocent-like. This girl was as much trouble as a pound of hungry puppies. "You already said our waitress isn't the one, so let's find your true love. Maybe Dolly Parton here can help with a little matchmaking magic."

Ooph. Why did this Ciara's comment that she wasn't Taika's true love make her want to punch something? If he wasn't interested in her, he wasn't. But the diner was a weird place to try to meet someone. This wasn't exactly a Tinder hotspot. "Oh, no. I don't think so. I'm better at singing and bringing food than any matchmaking."

"Come on now, chook. We've got a connection. You'll be great at helping me find my guy or gal, he, she, or they." Taika got a sexy kind of twinkle in his eye that had her wishing she was the one who had a blind date with him. "I can't exactly tell you why, but I think whoever it is might be here right now."

Guy or gal? She both liked him even more and was even more disappointed. He was pan but not attracted to her. She just couldn't win.

All the girls turned their heads and stared at him. Ciara was the first to quit just outright staring. "Why didn't you say so?"

She scooted right out of the booth and went over to the nearest table, pulling a woman still holding her fork full of pancakes in her hand. "How about her?"

Taika sniffed and shook his head. Ciara narrowed her eyes at him. "You're sure? You didn't have a clue last night and like I said, you're, umm, glowing."

"I'm sure." He looked directly at her, even though he was talking to his friends. "I'll know it when I know it."

This was the strangest bunch of people Lena had ever

had the pleasure of waiting on. "I'll just go get your orders in. Let me know if I can help with anything else."

Taika gave her a smile and a nod, but Ciara ignored her all together. She pushed pancake girl back to her table and grabbed the next closest person. "Him?"

"Hey, let me go."

"Nope. He's not the one."

A song she just had to sing popped into Lena's head. She hummed the tune as she turned in the order, then flipped on the karaoke machine, hopped up on the bar, and started singing something completely different. No way was she belting out *I Will Always Love You* while making goo goo eyes at Taika. He'd told his gal pals he wasn't interested in her.

Fine. She'd just have to be content with sex dreams about him. The crowd whooped and hollered as she sang the opening lines to Dolly's pop hit, *Here You Come Again.*

And later tonight, that's exactly what she'd be doing while she thought about him.

SHIFTER OLYMPICS

Ciara and the other mates had dragged almost every person in the diner in front of him, until the Wyverns decided the girls were pushing the boundaries of exposing them to the humans with the shenanigans. At this point he didn't even want to find his mate. Okay, that was a lie, but the search was fricking exhausting. Was this how other Dragon Warriors who didn't have a finding sense felt like all the time?

"Hello, Earth to Taika. Can you make that happen for the opening ceremonies?" Steele, the Second Wyvern of the Green Dragons, punched him in the arm.

The five Seconds were in charge of the opening ceremonies and at the ladies' insistence, they'd been delayed to tonight instead of this morning so everyone could witness his embarrassment at not being able to find his mate.

"Sorry, bro. Tell me again what you want me to do."

Since he'd been the last Second to arrive, he hadn't been in on the plans for their display of elemental powers.

Dax, who was always way too happy for a Red, gave his bestie Steele, the Green Second, a look and they both chuckled and shook their heads. They had no idea what it was like not to be able to find a mate. Dax met his and mated her in less than twenty-four hours. No wonder he was constantly happy go lucky.

"I know what it's like to be wrapped up in mate drama." Gris, the Gold's Second might be one of the only Dragon Warriors who did sort of understand what Taika was going through. He'd had his mate literally stolen by the Succubus Queen before they got to complete the mating ritual. "So, we'll keep it real simple and easy for you. You've seen the humans' Olympics, right?"

"Sure. Kiwi's kick ass at rowing." They'd dominate all the summer Olympic sports if Blue Dragons were allowed to compete.

"Olympics?" Neo, the newest of the Seconds and the only other one without a mate, had lived in Hell most of his life and was still learning about human culture.

"Yeah. Athletic competitions. Like our shifter trials, but with their human restrictions of muscles and stamina," Gris explained.

Neo nodded and motioned for Zon to continue. He was already privy to the plans for the opening ceremonies anyway.

"We'll be displaying our prowess with our elements by forming a symbol similar to the Olympic rings in the sky above the playing field. They'll stay up for the duration of the games."

"Yeah, I can do that. Just tell me when and where."

"You're kicking it off as soon as you're ready. Blue is the first ring, so the element of water is up first. Unless of course you've got somewhere else to be." Steele waggled his eyebrows. They all knew Taika did in fact have somewhere else to be. But the first shifter games of his lifetime was a big deal. It was more than just some competitions. It represented the first time in generations that the Dragons weren't at war with Hell and could kick back and have a little fun.

"Where I need to be is at the finish line of the elemental obstacle course after kicking your ass, greenie." They all had competitive streaks and while Taika had this mate search hanging over his head, he did have an obligation to represent his Wyr.

But what Taika really needed was a nice long dip in the water. Or even better, a dip between his lover's legs. Too bad not a single soul in these fates forsaken hills seemed to be the one true mate for him. Now that his soul shard had lit up, he wasn't interested in a dalliance with anyone else. Ever.

Didn't mean he wasn't still a walking hard-on. He'd had to keep his menu over his lap the whole time they'd been in the diner. Yet still his mate evaded him. But why? Couldn't whoever they were feel the pull to him?

He was completely convinced either his soul shard was broken, or he was.

Because if it had nothing to do with fate, and he could pick his own mate, he'd go for the delightful plump waitress at the diner. He'd instantly felt protective of her last night when he sensed those asshats were making her uncomfortable, and he could definitely imagine losing himself in all those curves. But clearly the universe was playing a cruel joke on him since he couldn't be within two feet of her without sneezing his face off.

Taika had never sneezed so much in his life. He'd spent a fair amount of time making fun of humans when they caught their colds or had their allergies. Dragons didn't get either, so this was a new one on him. See? Broken.

Fuck.

If they hadn't only just defeated Ereshkigal and sent her back to the underworld, he'd think she was at work here, trying to steal his mate for her own nefarious purposes.

"Let's get this show on the road, boys. Last one with their ring in the sky is a rotten wyrm." Taika shifted with a running jump and lifted up into the sky. He flew up just to the edge of the wards put in place by the local coven of witches especially for the games. Humans wouldn't be able to see or hear anything happening inside the wards and would feel compelled to avoid the area.

He pulled some water droplets out of the sky, more from some small streams, and even more from a lake that he could feel nearby but was also hidden by some kind of magic. His blue ring of water formed easily, and cheers went up from the contingent of Blue Dragon Warriors gathered on the playing field below.

He'd never held a trick like this up for days on end, but his affinity and power over the element was so deep in his being that it would be simple enough. Like remembering to brush his teeth before bed. Something he had to consciously do but didn't take a whole lot of mental capacity.

The other rings went up, and he had to admit, it was fucking cool to see how his fellow dragons used their own elements to make their rings appear. Especially Neo's power over shadow. Black Dragons were still a bit of a novelty, and he never would have understood how shadow was an element if he hadn't seen how they used it in the final battle with Hell.

Once Dax lit the red ring on fire with a snort, they all landed on the field, shifted back to their human forms, and took a bow. The crowd flipped out and it wasn't because of what he and the other Seconds had done. The five of them looked up to where many were pointing, and their five elemental rings were being encircled by an intensely colorful rainbow.

The First Dragon was here, and he was putting his blessing on them all. Sweet as. Just knowing the mythical father of all Dragonkind was watching over them lifted Taika's heart. Maybe the games would be the distraction he needed to not sink into being a grumpy old dragon like Match had been before he'd found Fallyn.

That guy had been one scary son of an alpha. Taika

was already cranky enough this week, especially for a Blue Dragon Warrior.

If the First Dragon was here, perhaps his mate, the White Witch, mother of dragons, was too, and she was infamous for helping her children find their mates. She was the goddess of love after all.

Cage, who'd been their AllWyvern during the battles with Hell, raised his arms into the air and used his power over the wind like a megaphone. "Let the trials begin."

With his words, the elemental obstacle course appeared on the field and man, was this going to be a challenge. He'd be watching his fellow Blue Dragon Warriors closely until it was his turn to see if he couldn't get a few strategies to work through the other elements.

The first round lined up in their dragon forms and waited for the starting signal. With a bang from Cage's lightning bolt, they started off. The Blue was a young Dragon Warrior not yet in his prime. He kept right up with the Gold, flying in the first obstacle of the windstorm, got a bit lost in the shadow, but sped ahead in the waves of water suspended just above the ground. He and the Green were neck and neck as they hit the wall of earth, and he narrowly avoided the vines slashing out trying to wrap around him.

But then he hit the fire element obstacle. The floor was literally lava. The kid really gave it a go. He used his power over water to turn much of it to rock, but the fire broke though, and spires of molten magma burst up, knocking him off course with the heat and steam. Even a last-minute shield of ice didn't protect him for long, and the Green Dragon Warrior slipped past him to get to the finish line first.

"Good job, kid. That was a great run." Taika shouted to the disappointed Blue. He really did mean the praise, but to any good warrior, second place was never good enough. He was now better armed with how hard that damn fire obstacle would be.

The course reset, so as to be fair to each round of trials. This time the fire obstacle was first, and the Blue Dragon barely made it through. He had to limp through the rest of the course and the Green Dragon medics had to fix him up with some of their healing Dragon's Breath before he retreated to the small pond they set up for the blues' healing station. He'd be right as rain in a few minutes, but yikes, that fire obstacle was no joke.

Three more rounds of the course with one Gold, another Green, and a Red Dragon taking the first-place spots. The Seconds were all expected to compete, although not the Wyverns themselves. But one thing that Taika noticed as he observed each round, the dragons with mates fared better overall. Only one winner, the Black Dragon called Ace, of trial number two, was unmated.

Huh. One more reason to go searching for his mate after today's games. Not like he needed a reason, but he wouldn't mind getting to show off his prowess for his brand-new lover and soul mate. Even better if he won and they could celebrate with a mating ritual and some bedroom games.

Taika stretched from his place on the sidelines and psyched himself up for his run at the elements. He pounded on his chest and let his favorite haka chant run through his head. If his head had been in the game and not on finding his mate, or that waitress's thick thighs, he might have led his fellow Blue Dragon Warriors in the haka before this first trial.

He'd make sure they did one tomorrow for the second trial of the games. Not only did he and the boys live for celebrating their Māori heritage, but bonus, it always freaked the other Wyrs out, as was the intention. With Blues' easy-going attitude, no one expected the war cries and intimidating faces.

He shifted and lined up with the other Seconds as they prepared for the final heat of the elemental obstacle course trial.

Thinking of the Haka also had him remembering all the ones they'd done to celebrate mating rituals this year. He could hardly wait to do one for his mate. Assuming they were an American, they may not even have a clue about the intricate history of the ceremonial dance. He could hardly wait to show them.

Ky's voice popped into his head. *"Uh, hello. Bro, are you going to do the trial, or are you going to stand there with your tail up your ass?"*

Shit. He hadn't even heard the bang of the lightning to start the race. Taika leaned into his element hard to help him catch up. He used the water to create a watery tunnel straight through the first trial of Earth, turned the windstorm into rain to help him speed through the Wind element, and rode a long wave in a body surf through the shadow because water didn't get lost, dragons did.

By the time he popped out of the shadow, he was neck and neck with Dax. Only fire and water were left, so one of them would win and the other was going down.

He'd watched his fellow Blues use their element to battle the fire, and each had struggled. He planned to embrace the coming together of the two elements and let that propel him to victory. Taika pulled up every ounce of water he could get his hands on and pushed it out in one huge rocket of a stream. He skimmed along the front edge, waiting for the fire to take over.

The moment the two elements clashed, the water turned to scalding steam. It was hot, but it was still a form of water, and he rode that burst of steam all the way through the elemental obstacle until he splashed down into the cool water of the final leg of the trail.

The water enhanced all of his senses and that was the moment that Taika noticed the darkness lurking at the edge of the field of play. Whoever, or whatever, it was didn't belong here. There was something deeply wrong about it. Before he could even send out an alarm, the ugly feeling he sensed receded, and a man and woman stumbled out of the trees where the darkness was and onto the field.

Taika shot to the edge of the woods to get to them,

with all four of the other Seconds close behind him. He wasn't the only one who knew when to play a game and when to protect the world from the forces of evil. Whatever that had been was definitely wicked and villainous.

The woman, who had the scent of a witch, stumbled and fell to her knees, her eyes blank and her jaw slack. She was still breathing, still alive, but it was as if she had nothing going on inside of her brain. What in the fuck just happened to her? The man dropped to the ground beside her, staring up at the sky, but seeing nothing.

Steele grabbed the woman first and breathed his healing breath on her, but nothing changed. He looked to the rest of them, but none had an answer to what had happened. The Wyverns ran over with their mates, who were all powerful elemental witches in their own rights. They were the ones who'd worked with the local coven to secure the area in the first place.

Fallyn, who was the direct descendant of a strong line of Red Witches, the kind that helped pull a piece of a dragon's soul into his shard, took one look at the witch and gasped. "She... has no soul."

Without even needing to think, Taika knew. "There was an evil here right before the witches appeared. It has done something malevolent with their souls. I don't know what, but it's definitely chaotic and evil."

Taika sneezed. Why did he smell rhubarb pancakes and hot sauce?

MY MAMA ALWAYS SAID LIFE WAS LIKE A BOX OF DRAGONS

What stunk the most about living in a small town is that everybody knows your business. Since she worked both of the busiest weekend shifts, Lena had every Friday off at the diner, but it wasn't a day for relaxing. She couldn't even pretend to be sick to stay in and eat pizza and ice cream and veg out watching a movie on her couch all day because then three neighbors, the county sheriff, and Billy would all be sent to check on her.

It wasn't like she was going to go to the Rhubarb Festival today either.

So that meant the inevitable visit to Mama's.

She loved her mama. She really did. It was just that her mama was mean as a rabid badger most days and the ones when she wasn't, the world was only sadness and grief. Lena hadn't really known her dad, but there were days when she hated him for dying and breaking Mama's heart into so many pieces that trying to pick them all back up again was too much.

"Mama, I'm here." Lena opened the squeaky screen door just off the kitchen and let it slam shut nice and loud to warn her mother of her presence. Even though she called out, sometimes nothing but the loud bang got her attention. It wasn't like anyone else would be visiting, but her mother's anxiety was a funny business. "I got the brisket and potato salad you like from the Satterfields over in Gatlinburg."

It was always smart to come with a peace offering to butter her mom up with, and food was usually a winner. Except of course, anything rhubarb. Mama was even suspicious of strawberry pie during the season.

"Why'd you drive all the way over to Gatlinburg?" she hollered from the front room. "That's a waste of gasoline if I ever heard one."

"Yes, ma'am." She put the food in the icebox because there was no way they would eat it now. It wasn't going to be a good visit then. Hopefully Mama had some errands she needed Lena to run, and she could escape. Maybe she had a casserole dish to return to Dixie Sue who lived next door. One could only hope.

"And don't you send that boy from the pharmacy over here again. He was looking at me funny."

Probably because she hadn't brushed her hair or put on a bra in the last fourteen years. "I'm sure he didn't mean no disrespect. Just trying to do his job."

There was a little too long of a pause while her

mother considered that. "I don't like him, and I won't have him on my property, you hear me? You can ask Dixie Sue or her husband to go for me instead. They're cousins of ours you know."

Lena walked to the doorway and stood there for a minute, looking into the living room. It wasn't as big a mess as usual. Just a few coffee mugs. She hoped Mama had more to eat than coffee and sugary creamer all week. "Yes, ma'am. I know, and I will."

"Don't you yes, ma'am me when you don't mean it." Mama patted the arm of the seventies rust-colored, floral print couch. "Now come over here and let me look at you."

Oh gawd. Not this again. Lena looked around for anything else that needed doing. There'd be a fit if she tried to pick up the dishes and do them now, but she literally couldn't think of any other excuse not to come sit down on the couch.

It didn't matter whether she lost weight or gained weight, dyed her hair blonde, brown, pink, or aquamarine, wore make-up or not, her mother would nitpick something and tell her that's why she wasn't married yet.

"Have you put on weight?"

It didn't matter, it didn't matter. It. Did. Not. Matter. "No."

"You should." Mama made a harumph sound. "That Billy likes a woman with a little meat on her bones. You've seen how his eyes have been a roving over Dixie Sue now that she's big as a house."

Literally last week, Mama had told her he liked women with svelte figures. Who even said svelte anymore? "Mama, I'm not interested in marrying Billy, and he's not interested in me."

"He's a nice normal boy and he might be interested if you fattened up a little bit for him. Go get out that brisket and we'll have some." She waved Lena away like a servant. And Lena stood to do as she was told. It was just easier that way.

At least if they were eating, she could try to bring up the therapist in Knoxville who specialized in agoraphobia that would do the telehealth sessions. "I'll eat if you'll agree to talk to the therapist."

"Don't you think you can blackmail me." She punctuated her words with a good finger wagging. "I'm not talking to some head shrinker just because you don't want to come over here and take care of your own mother."

Sigh. "No, ma'am. I'm just trying to get you some help."

Her mother's face went from angry to sad in a half a second flat. She teared up and reached up to cup Lena's face in her palm. Her voice was quiet and calm and caring. "I know, baby. I'm just not there yet, okay. I'm trying but I... can't."

It was moments like this that kept Lena coming back. She'd stopped catering to her mama's every mean streak to protect her own mental health quite a few years back, and it had been really hard to set those boundaries. But it still hurt her heart that her mother couldn't find peace.

"Okay, Mama. Just keep trying. Think about talking to the therapist. You don't have to actually talk to her yet, but think about it."

"I'll try, child." Mama turned on the TV, which was her main coping mechanism on the daily, and put it to an old movie station. Best Little Whorehouse in Texas was just starting, and they sat together and watched it. It was one of the nicest mornings Lena had spent with her mother in years.

Until of course, the movie was over and real life was back. Lena picked up the mugs and took them to the sink to wash them out. Mama slapped some papers around and swore a blue streak about not being able to find the book she was looking for. This was always how her fits started. Losing her temper over the trivial things because she didn't feel like she had any control over the important things in her life.

Lena seriously considered sneaking out just to avoid the inevitable confrontation. But she wouldn't. She'd grin and bear it, and make sure her mother knew at least one person in the world loved her.

"Lena. Lena." Her mama hustled into the kitchen, but not to pick a fight. "Billy's here. I just saw his car pull up. He can't be visiting Dixie Sue, they ain't home. He must be here for you then. Do you have a date with him?"

Crappy crackers. Why the hell was he at her mama's?

"No, ma'am. I told you we aren't seeing each other. I don't know why he's here."

Even if he was looking for Lena, he wouldn't come to her mama's house. She scowled at his car from the screen door. She couldn't think of a single good reason why he'd be in this neighborhood. He still lived with his parents in their big house over on the diner's side of town.

He didn't even get out of his car. Just left it running, sitting there with the A/C on, staring at the house. She wrinkled her nose and had to force herself to straighten up her face in case he could see her. Billy had never been her favorite person in town, there was always something a little bit dark about him that turned her off. But he'd never been outright creepy and stalkery.

"Hold on now, who is that man coming up the walk? You aren't cheating on Billy with that man that looks like a Chip and Dales stripper, are you?"

Lena had never once stolen anyone's man. She would never cheat or ask anyone else to cheat. Just because her name was Jolene, didn't mean she was going to steal anyone's man.

"No, Mama. I'm not seeing Billy, and I don't think that man is a stripper. I served him at the diner a couple of times. He's here for a family reunion or something." She'd like to be that something.

But what in the world was he doing coming up her mama's front walk? And why was he sniffing everything? And where did those lawn gnomes come from?

"Who has a family reunion in Walker Valley? People

who need to hide from prying eyes, that's who. But Lawd-a-mercy if I wasn't a married woman, I'd jump his bones. Don't you go near that man, you hear me, Jolene Margaret Walker?"

Geez Louise. A. Her mama wasn't married, she was widowed and could jump anyone's bones she liked. And B., now Lena was going to have dirty images of Taika stripping. But also, of her mother shoving dollar bills down his pants. That was bad. So unbelievably bad.

Taika stared through the screen door, did a double take, and sneezed. "Dolly?"

"Uh, hi." She smoothed her hair down and folded her arms across her chest. She wasn't all gussied up like she did for work. Not that it should matter. He'd already decided he wasn't interested in her. And why was she even thinking about any of that? He was standing in her mother's front yard acting weird, not here to ask her out. "It's Lena actually. Can I help you?"

He glanced around the yard like there was something fishy going on. "This is going to sound really strange, trust me, I know. But I think you're in trouble and I'd like you to come with me. I'll keep you safe."

Ohhkay. Had anyone else in the whole entire universe said that she'd think they were at best, pulling a scam and at worst, trying to kidnap her. No way she'd end up putting the lotion on her skin so she didn't get the hose again. It was both strange and right that she trusted Taika. For no good reason, but she trusted her gut. "Safe from what?"

"I just realized that sounds serial killery." He sneezed again, but his reaction to her didn't seem as severe as at the diner. "Sorry, I don't mean to. This isn't going to help, but that what is not going to be easy to explain."

Mama came over and poked her face in between Lena and the screen door. "What do you want, young man? You ain't from around here, are ya? You keep your business to yourself, you hear me?"

"Sorry," she mouthed to Taika. "Mama, he's trying to be helpful. Don't be rude."

An old hoot owl dive bombed off Mama's roof at Billy's car and he must have decided there was too much trouble to be had, because he peeled out and drove away. What an asshat.

Her mother didn't even budge. Instead, she pushed her face against the screen and whispered to Lena. "There's something funny about that man that I don't trust. He reminds me of your daddy."

What? He looked nothing like the one picture her mama kept hidden in her nightstand of the two of them when they were young. Lena wasn't even supposed to know that picture existed. That was the first time she could remember Mama saying anything about her father.

Taika stepped closer to the screen door and Lena's necklace went crazy. So did Taika's nose. It was as if someone had blown pepper in his face.

"What in tarnation is wrong with the two of you? I don't like it. Lena, you get on back home and you tell that tall, dark, handsome stranger to get off my lawn." Her mama high-tailed it back into the living room and while Lena expected to hear the blare of the TV, instead she heard the slam of the bedroom door.

At least she was going to get out of spending the rest of the morning with her mother. Lena stepped out of the house and quietly shut the door behind her. Her necklace was buzzing so hard she grabbed it and shoved it inside of her shirt just so he wouldn't think she had on a wearable vibrator and then walked out into the yard to meet him.

Taika sniffed and then stepped closer. He towered over her and yet they fit together exactly right. Silly. He didn't like her that way. She tilted her head back a little to look up at him and he was already staring down at her. His eyes twinkled and Lena couldn't help but lick her lips.

"Are you okay?" He was so close, his voice wasn't more than a whisper and she didn't need more than that. The words skittered over her just like a caress.

"Yes?" That shouldn't be a question. He just had her so flustered. She couldn't pay attention to what she was supposed to say, only the way his chest rose and fell as he sucked all the air out of her universe.

"You sure, chook?" If she'd thought his eyes were twinkling before, she was wrong. The deep blue might actually be made of real-life stars.

"No." What were they talking about?

"What is it about you, Lena? I can't stop thinking about you, and I was absolutely drawn to your little diner, and this house, because of you. But I should know if... Are you some kind of a witch who's cast a spell on me?"

"A sneezing spell?" They were so close she could smell the salty, briny scent of his skin.

His sneezing, sniffling fit he had every time he was around her seemed to have gone away. "Stranger spells than that have been known to afflict people like me."

Taika leaned in closer, and his gaze flitted from her eyes to her mouth and back again.

Oh, please, oh please, oh puhleeze just freaking kiss her. She'd never ask for anything ever again if he would just kiss her. She let her body sway towards him, closing the last ten percent gap. "And what kind of people are those?"

The screen squeaked behind her, and she heard a telltale chock-chock of a double-barreled shotgun being locked and loaded. "The dragon kind."

Lena spun to see her mother pointed the old gun that was about as big as her right at Taika. "Mama! What are you doing?"

"Get away from him, Jolene. He's a dragon and dragons are what killed your daddy."

SEEK AND YOU SHALL FIND

Shit. Wasn't he just having a mare today? First the dark presence and the catatonic witches, now Lena's mum both pegged him as a Dragon Warrior and had a shotgun pointed at his chest.

To top it all off, he wanted to snog the hell out of a woman who was not his fated mate. What the fuck, bro?

When he'd identified that hot sauce and rhubarb pancake smell, he'd freaked the piss out that somehow his favorite curvy waitress was involved in some evil activities. Even more so when he saw her in the house where the presence was lurking.

But he was still standing here with her, and the dark presence was gone. It wasn't her or her mother. But what if it had been seeking them out to hurt them in the same way it had done those witches? It may have already affected her mum, because this woman had a crazy look in her eye, and it wasn't the only thing aimed at him.

"Mama, you put that gun down right this instant. Don't make me call the police and have them drag you off to the looney bin." She put herself in between him and the gun and Taika's heart skipped so many beats, it might as well explode.

Lena clearly wasn't scared of her mother, but Taika was. He wouldn't let her ever be harmed, and especially not to protect him. He moved around Lena and held out his hands trying to placate the crazy lady. "I'm not going to hurt you or your daughter, ma'am. You've got nothing to be afraid of."

He didn't deny her accusation that he was a Dragon. He'd lie to protect the secret of Dragonkind's existence from humans if he had to, but only as a last resort. What he really had to find out was how or why this human woman even knew of Dragons in the first place, and how the hell she knew he was one. "What makes you think I'm a dragon, love?"

"Don't you come another step closer." The fear and confusion flittered through her eyes. She might be a bit off her rocker, but there was knowledge and intelligence in there too. This woman had seen a thing or two. "I know what you did to my Chrysós. Don't you be thinking you can take his daughter too."

Chrysós sure didn't sound like an American name. In fact, he knew a few Gold Dragon Warriors called that. But if Lena was a dragon's daughter, he would scent it on her.

"Mama. I'm serious. If you don't put that gun down right this instant, I'm gonna come over there and take it from you." Lena didn't wait for her mother to respond. She jumped out and grabbed the barrel of the shotgun, pointing it toward the ground and wrestling it out of her mother's grip.

"You don't know what you're doing, child." The woman threw her hands up in the air and huffed away, slamming her way back into the house.

If she was sincerely worried he'd hurt her daughter, she wouldn't have backed down. So, some of that was for show. Or a test. He hoped he'd passed. Except, it shouldn't matter, because Lena was not his fated mate.

Ky's voice popped into his head. *"We've made progress on the mystery of the witches who stumbled into the games. Return to the mountain so we can fill you in, but it appears to be a local affair and all's well. We'll be able to finish the trials."*

Hmm. He wasn't yet ready to leave Lena, and he could give a piss about the games. *"I'll be up as soon as I can. I've had an encounter in the town that might be related. There's a woman here who seems to know about the Dragon Warriors."*

"Interesting. Keep me advised, but head back soon. The group is anxious to continue the games." Ky's tone was far from worried, and that calmed Taika more than anything else. His Wyvern was ever vigilant and if he said there was no threat, he meant it.

Lena blew out a long, pent-up breath. "I'm so sorry about my mama. She's had a rough time of it since my dad died. Which, truth be told, is a pretty long time. I don't think she would have hurt you, but she might be worse off than I thought seeing as she's talking about dragons."

"Sorry about your dad, chook. Is this talk of the paranormal something new for her?" Maybe her mother had already been affected by the darkness he sensed and that's why he'd been drawn here in his investigation.

"She's not on drugs or anything. At least I don't think she is. I don't know where she'd even get them if she was." Lena rubbed her forehead and he wanted to make everything all better for her. He was this close to reaching out and kissing that exact spot on her head. "Except for the couple of times I've gone on vacation, I get all of her groceries and her medications. Anyway, sorry again."

Lena looked down at her feet and kicked at a piece of dirt on the ground. "This is a small town and I'm sure some neighbor will be spreading rumors real quick, but I'd appreciate it if you didn't say anything about this to anyone."

Fuck. She was dealing with her mother's mental illness all on her own, and it didn't sound like she had any support. He wanted to wrap her right up into his arms and tell her everything was going to be okay. But was it? She was putting distance between them both physically and mentally, and he didn't like it one bit. She needed someone in the world who cared about her so she could keep caring about her mother.

Taika moved right up into her space and lifted her

chin. Just touching her made his whole body vibrate with need. He wanted to kiss her so damn bad right now. He couldn't do that to whoever his mate might be. Why wasn't it her? “Some of the others I'm here with, my family, are good with healing. I'd be happy to ask them to come by and see your mum.”

Every other Dragon Warrior explicitly said they knew immediately when they found their fated mate. Except of course, Jakob, since Ciara was the one who had to break the curse. He would know if it was Lena. He would know.

Several thoughts flitted through his mind. If his soul shard was broken, which it clearly was, did it matter what fate wanted?

“Thanks, but that would probably send her into all kinds of fits. She doesn't deal well with new situations.” Her eyes glistened, and those tears were ripping his soul out. She pulled away and wouldn't look at him anymore and he hated it. Hated every damn second.

“I'm gonna go check in on her, so, if you're still around, I guess I'll maybe see you at the diner.” She was trying to politely tell him to bugger off and he knew it.

So why didn't he just leave? Ky had called him back, she was done with him, and his feet were glued to this damn sidewalk. “I'd like that. When are you working again?”

“Not until tomorrow thankfully.” She glanced inside the house and moved her body, making ready to go inside.

Never once in his life had he been this awkward with

someone he wanted. He shouldn't even be interested in her in the first place. This had to be punishment by the First Dragon for some kind of fuck up on his part. "Okay. I'll, uh, we'll be sure to stop in."

She waved him off and disappeared inside, but not before glancing back, giving him the most mournful look. Taika sent up a silent prayer to the First Dragon and the White Witch. *Please help me find my fated mate soon and, while I know it isn't her, please let it be Lena.*

Taika jogged toward the mountain and then shifted into his dragon form to fly back up under the cover of the magical wards that hid him from human eyes. The moment the shift took him over, he got a tingling feeling all through his scales and his soul shard went berserk. He swore that he heard a voice inside his head that was not his Wyvern nor any other member of his Wyr.

You got it, kid.

Then a second voice that was unrecognizable, but also so familiar. *Douchepotato.*

That had to be his fellow competitors trying to get into his head before the next trial. He and the other Second Wyverns had already all forfeited the first trial for not finishing. If he wanted to win the games, he would have to try harder. His Wyr would have to get better at their mind games to throw him off.

When he landed on the field, he caught the very end of the Blue Dragon Warriors performing a Haka. Damn. He'd hoped to lead them. He was glad someone in the ranks had taken the initiative though. Good on them. He'd be sure to be here to participate in the next one. Especially after the morning he'd had. He could use some letting loose and pouring his emotions and frustrations into a good old war chant.

Ky made one more grunt and a face at the crowd along with the rest of the lot and then trotted over to greet Taika. "Glad you're back, bro. Turns out the coven of witches in this area has been around for a long time and there are some old feuds between the descendants of the Walker family."

"Walker. Sounds familiar. Bugger. I think that's the family name of the woman I just met who accused me of being a Dragon."

Ky tipped his head, thinking. "I'll have to check in with the coven about her then. We'll follow up after the games."

Cage moved to the center of the field again and announced the next trial. "Gather round, Dragon Warriors, you're going to get a kick out of this next game. The Wyvern Mates came up with it and it's a doozy."

Uh-oh. Anything the mates are involved in was sure to be interesting.

"This is a search and find trial."

What? Three quarters of the Dragon Warriors groaned, and several voices expressed their discontent. "Jada must have bribed the other mates with her baked goods."

"Yeah, this is clearly a round of Blues Clues. Come on."

Cage grinned and held up his hands to quiet the complainers. "I know, I know, this sounds like it's made for our friends who are blue, but never underestimate our lovely mates. They've figured out exactly how to level the playing field."

Everyone went silent waiting for the rub. Cage played it out as long as he could before everyone started razzing him. He was loving every minute of it. When the cheers and razzes got to concert level, Cage finally gave in and announced the rules of the trial.

"You'll be searching for an incredibly special item. A dragon's egg."

Oohs and ahhs sounded throughout the crowd. Dragon's eggs had been used by the Wyverns for centuries to house the most sacred treasures and relics from their hoards. It was said they were remnants from when the first sons of the First Dragon were born, but Taika was sure that was a load of bunk since Dragon Warriors were born of women, who definitely did not lay big golden eggs.

"Ciara and Yvaine have cooked up a little magic that makes whatever you put inside the egg the perfect gift for your fated mate."

Taika's chest went icy cold. Was this another test from the universe to prove his soul was broken? It had to be. Yeah, no. He'd be bowing out of this trial, and that meant he was forfeiting his chance to be the Dragon

Trials champion. A younger, unmated dragon near the front voiced that very concern. "What if we don't have a mate?"

The five Wyverns looked at each other and they were all smiles. Cage once again answered for them. "We have it on the highest authority that every Dragon Warrior does, in fact, have a fated mate."

Even if they were sure they were broken or cursed?

Cage looked directly at Taika. "Everyone."

That sent quite an excited murmur through the crowd. He wanted so much for that to be true. The Wyverns were known to have contact with the spirits of the First Dragon and the White Witch, and if that was the authority they spoke of, it had to be true.

Maybe he wasn't broken after all. Just really bad at finding his one true mate.

"Wait. How are you going to make it fair to those of us who aren't blessed with the Blues' gift of finding?"

Azy, Cage's sassy mate, stepped up next to him, looking very queenly and benevolent. "Because you'll be doing this trial as humans. No elemental or other shiftery senses or powers allowed."

Taika literally snort laughed. Well, that was one way to silence a crowd of rowdy Dragons. The lot of them were dumbfounded. Not since he'd gotten his soul shard just before puberty had he done anything without his dragon at the front and center. None of them had. They'd be like little kids wandering around in the dark.

"And just to make sure no one cheats," Azy continued,

"We've prepared a special spell for the duration of this trial."

She signaled to Ciara and Fallyn, who were the most powerful elemental witches of the Wyverns' mates. Ciara swirled her fingers over her head and right there in the middle of the summer afternoon, it began to snow. But these were no ordinary snowflakes. Fallyn closed her eyes, lifted her palms to the sky and the snowflakes glowed and shimmered with all the colors of the rainbow. They reminded Taika of Christmas ornaments.

"Whoever intends to compete for this once in a lifetime opportunity at a Dragon's egg, reach up and grab a snowflake. But know that until the egg is found, you won't be able to shift or use your power over the elements."

At first no one reached for a snowflake, and Taika decided he wasn't going to miss this chance. He only cared a little about the egg. Something deep inside of him said that finding the perfect gift hidden inside the egg would bring him to his fate, to his one true love.

The moment he touched the snowflake, his vision went fuzzy, and his knees went weak. Huh. Was this what humans felt like all the time? When the other competitors had taken their snowflakes, the Wyverns pointed them to a starting line.

"The Wyverns and those not competing will patrol the playing field, which includes the forested area all within the witches' wards. The first person to recover the dragon's egg wins and the spell keeping you from shifting and using your senses and powers will be broken. Good luck and may the First Dragon bless you."

With that, Cage popped off his lightning that acted as their starting gun and Taika took off into the forest. Where he promptly smacked right into the side of an enormous, rainbow-scaled Dragon. *About damn time you got here, douchepotato.*

YOUR LOVE IS BETTER THAN SCHMOONSHINE

Fuck it. After the nightmare day she had, Lena needed to blow off some steam. She was going to the god damned Rhubarb Festival. She was going to have strawberry rhubarb pie, have a rhubarb slushy, and maybe even try the very strange sounding rhubarb barbecue ribs.

Rhubarb everything.

How did her mother even know she was allergic to it, if she'd never had it?

She was going to find out, and also secretly hope the EMTs working the festival had an epi-pen handy in case she was wrong.

But she'd been hit with that rhubarb pie the other day and hadn't broken out in hives or had her throat close up. Allergic schmallergic.

She'd stayed until almost dusk with her mama before she was comfortable leaving her on her own. And she took the shotgun home with her and hid it underneath her bed. Then she took a shower and gussied herself right up. She was going to have fun if it killed her.

It might.

In her best boots and her hair Dolly Parton big, she strolled into the center of town, which was only a few blocks from her place. Since she'd always avoided the festival, she was awed by how fun and cute the two blocks that they cordoned off looked. There were pink and red lights, a whole row of booths with all kinds of great smelling food, and weird merchandise for sale.

The part she'd been looking forward to the most was the music tent. She headed straight for it, waving to people and saying hi.

She'd set on her front porch for years and listened to the bands who rolled through every year, wishing she could go on down and join them. Well, tonight she was going to. Maybe she'd even get up on stage with them. That would show her mama.

Urgh. Which was not what she wanted to do. Her mama was doing the best she could. Mental illness was a bitch and a half, and Lena knew better than to be mad at her mama for something she couldn't control. Didn't mean it wasn't hard on them both though.

She just needed to have a little fun and let her wild out tonight, and her mother didn't need to be any the wiser. Tomorrow everything would be right as rain. She popped into the back of the music tent and one of her many cousins, or cousins of cousins twice removed, or whatever they were, waved her over to their table.

"Hey, have you seen Dixie Sue around?" she asked. "She hasn't popped yet, has she?"

Dix had been excited about the rhubarb festival for weeks. Said she'd been craving the rhubarb ribs and the pies something fierce. No one else in the family was allergic to rhubarb, so how could Lena be?

Dixie's side of the Walker family always had a booth with old timey remedies and such made from the mountain crop. Just the other day, she'd been going on about how they wouldn't let her have any to curb her cravings because they needed it for their tinctures and creams. Maybe she was over working the booth. Lena would check after she sang her song.

"Nope. Haven't seen her for days. She's nowhere to be found."

Yikes. "I hope she's alright."

"You know Walker Valley. We'd all poke our heads up like a bunch of prairie dogs if there was something wrong." Her cousin tapped her forehead indicating the idea that Walkers had some kind of sixth sense or something. Lena had never put much credence in the stories of some of her ancestors being mountain witches. What they thought of as a knowing power was nothing more than the local gossip train.

There was a real good band, and they were playing a Dolly Parton favorite, My Tennessee Mountain Home. They moved into the last chorus, and she sang along with everyone else, feeling better already. She never should have avoided coming down here every year. This was exactly the kind of thing she sought out when she went traveling. A place where people came together to be happy.

When the song was over, everyone clapped and the banjo player stepped up to the mic. "Thanks folks. Remember to open your wallets tonight, and help Dolly get some books out to kids who wanna read them."

Oh, they were supporting the Imagination Library tonight. That was so cool. There wasn't a kid under five in town who didn't get free books from Dolly every single month of the year. Her mama had signed her up the very first year Dolly started the program and Lena still had hers tucked away in a box somewhere, saving them for when she had kids of her own someday.

There weren't a whole lot of people who moved to put any money in the donation bin. Hmph. She'd stuck a whole roll of tip money from the someday jar into her bra to use for eating and drinking tonight. But she didn't need even half. Lena walked up front and peeled off the biggest bills and pushed them through the little slot into the big plexi box with the library's logo painted on the front.

"Well, lookie there, if it isn't Ms. Jolene Walker flaunting her money all about town." Billy sat alone at one of the picnic tables set up under the tent. The place was packed but it seemed like nobody wanted to sit with him.

"Care to do the same, Billy boy?" He hated being called that just as much as she disliked Leener Neener or Jolene.

"I'll put my money where your mouth is." He stared at her lips and licked his, trying to look sexy or something. It wasn't working. "Sing us a song and I'll donate something."

"You'll donate everything in your wallet, and don't be going and slipping it into your pocket to tell me you ain't got nothin'."

He scowled, but only because he knew she had him dead to rights. Funny that he wanted her to sing. He was usually the one who wanted to be in the spotlight. There was something else going on there. Lena glanced around the tent to see if there was anyone else from the diner she could commiserate with over Billy being such a dumbass, but she didn't see anyone.

"Fine, but I get to choose the song." He said it in a creepy way that had Lena scooting away. Why in the world her mother ever thought she would date this pile of poo was beyond her. Just having money wasn't enough for her. She wanted someone who cared about something besides themselves.

Lena went up the side steps and spoke quietly to the band. "Would you mind if I did a song? I promise I'm better than your average karaoke crooner."

The singer grinned and handed over the microphone. "I know who you are. I've eaten at the Grand Old Eatery most of my life. You're the best Dolly Parton they've ever had."

Wasn't that nice of her to say? "Thanks."

"What number do you want to do?" The banjo player, who must be the head of the group, asked. "We could use something to get the crowd riled up a bit. How about—"

Billy interrupted. "Jolene. Sing Jolene."

Great balls of fiery poop. She turned on him, but he had his hands cupped around his mouth and shouted out a chant. "Jolene, Jolene, Jolene."

The banjo player chuckled. "It's not like we don't all know that one by heart. Jolene it is."

Dammit. The guitar player started up with the first few chords before Lena could even protest. Ugh. If she was going to sing, she was gonna sing it right. Didn't matter if she hated this song, everyone else loved it.

She pulled her voice up from deep in her soul and let the haunting melody pour out of her. "Jolene, Jolene, Jolene, Jolee-een."

"Whoo! Sing it, Dolly," somebody in the back shouted out.

Every single person in the tent joined in until their voices burst out the sides and got carried away on the wind. That brought a whole lot more people into the tent. As the festival goers filtered in, most stopped by the donations box and dropped bills in. One woman even slipped some gold bracelets off and dropped them in too.

Wow, people were being generous now. Rock on.

As she rolled into the second verse about the cheater-pants man in the song talking in his sleep about her namesake, the tent was so full, she might have missed Taika bursting in.

Nope. No way she'd ever miss a sight like that. He was hot and sweaty like he'd run here just to see her perform. His chest was heaving and that interesting necklace he wore glowed, lighting up the inside of the tent with a soft blue light.

She sang that final verse about him being the only one for her right to him. For this one song only, he was her muse, and she was singing just for him. The crowd melted away, the other voices faded, and it was only him and her in the warm summer air, letting their hearts beat to the rhythm of the music.

It wasn't until she wailed the last mournful Jolee-een and the crowd erupted into hoots, hollers, and cheers that the spell between them was broken. A mass of people rushed up to the stage, but not to see her. They were shoving money into that donation bin faster than anything she'd ever seen.

Lena simply stood there, staring back at Taika. What was he doing here? Surely it wasn't because he was looking for her. He didn't like her that way. He'd said so.

The crowd thinned as many made their way back out to the rest of the festival. The band started up a new song, an instrumental piece, which was good, because she was still holding the mic, but did not have any breath left to sing with.

She handed the microphone back to the other singer

and stepped off the stage. Her feet didn't want to stop and led her right to within an inch of Taika. "Hi."

"Hi." He smiled down at her and his eyes were so blue, she was sure they were diamonds. He sniffled and rubbed his knuckles under his nose. But he didn't sneeze. "That's some set of golden pipes you've got there. I liked your song."

"Thanks. It's not my favorite, but it's a crowd pleaser. What are you doing here?" Yeah, she just blurted that out, like she was accusing him of something inappropriate.

"I'm looking for something. You look like you could use a drink. Can I buy you one?"

Her mouth had gone dry as an empty outhouse. "Uh, yeah. Great."

He stepped in beside her and placed his hand at the small of her back and guided her through the remaining crowd. Either her necklace was buzzing again, or her heart had gone into vibrator mode. On the high setting. That wasn't the only part of her body pulsing either. With just one touch, she was going to need new panties.

When they went past Billy, he scowled but shrunk away like he didn't want Taika to notice him. Taika sniffed the air and growled. She didn't imagine it this time. He. Growled.

Like a bear, or a wolf, or something bigger.

Billy didn't make any trouble though, and she was grateful that Taika just kept walking. He steered them toward the closest booth, which happened to be one serving local flavored moonshine. She didn't recognize the rainbow-colored logo that looked a lot like a garden gnome holding an egg with scales, or the proprietor, who was tall and lean with long hair and a prosthetic arm.

"Hello there, Mr. and Mrs. Potato Head. Can I tempt you with a sample of my schmoonshine?" Every syllable he said was like a laugh, and yet somehow completely serious at the same time.

She glanced up at Taika who shrugged and didn't say a word. But that smile told her he was down for some fun.

"Schmoonshine?" Was this even legal?

"Yeah. It is not Goddess of the Moon approved. I'm more a man of the sun and wind, anyway. You know what I mean? Here, try this cotton candy flavored one." He shoved a one-ounce cup into their hands and made the drink up motion with his thumb and pinky.

When in Rome, uh Rhubarb Festival. She and Taika clinked their plastic glasses, and they downed the little shooters in one go. While it made her eyes water, it was completely freaking delicious. "Wow. That was way better than I expected. What other flavors do you recommend? Don't you have a rhubarb one?"

"Oh, sweet potato flower, you don't want to try that one. It's just a gimmick." The striking woman dressed all in white at the ice cream booth next door leaned over the railing dividing the two stalls. Who wore all white to serve ice cream?

"Still, it is the rhubarb festival, and my first one in a long time, so I'd like to try it just the same, if you have it."

Taika shook his head. "None for me, thanks. Got anything oceany flavored?"

"One rhubarb schmoonshine, blech, and one seaweed schmoonshine, coming up." He poured two more little cups and handed them over.

Lena giggled. "Rhubarb is gross, but seaweed isn't?"

Taika tapped his cup against hers again. "Don't knock seaweed, it's one of my favorite flavors."

Gross. She was more of a coconut rum kind of gal. Beaches and cabana boys for the win. "Okay, then. Bottoms up."

Lena tossed this shot back just like the other one, and promptly spit it out all over Taika's shirt. "Oh my god, it burns, ugh. Gross. Help. Ack."

She swiped her hand over her tongue and fanned her mouth. Taika balked and looked around frantically for something to help her. The stall proprietor gave his head a tip to the side, indicating the ice cream stand. "Quick, give me a vanilla ice cream."

"Cup or a cone, child?" the woman in white asked as if he was any other customer ordering a treat.

Lena wanted to scream that it didn't matter, but her tongue was still on fire.

"Put it in..." He paused a minute, his spine went straight, and he stared into the booth slack jawed. What was he waiting for? "Put it in that umm, cup, right there, please."

"Ah, yes, the finders keepers cup. That's the last one on hand. Excellent choice." The woman scooped out a big dollop of ice cream and handed it over to Taika, grinning like she'd just served him the most delectable food in the universe.

He turned to her way too slowly and held the ice cream out to her in both hands. The ice cream was in a fancy souvenir cup that looked like a golden scaled egg. "Here's your gift, Lena. I hope it's the perfect one."

"Yeth, purfect-th." She grabbed the egg, didn't bother with the spoon, and stuck her tongue directly into the ice cream. The relief was instant. But her tongue wasn't the only thing that felt better. As she took the first bit of ice cream down her throat, she felt like a vice grip that she didn't even know had been wrapped around her chest, released. A shiver ran up and down her body and she blinked a fuzzy darkness out of her eyes.

Taika gasped and his necklace went supernova blue. "You are the one."

He whispered the words so reverentially that they were like a prayer. A prayer just for her. She looked up at him, seeing him like she never had before.

"You're a dragon." She dropped her ice cream, jumped into his arms, wrapping her legs around his waist, and kissed him. Kissed him like he was the first, last, and only man she ever wanted to be with. Forever.

MINE, FINALLY MINE

Lena was his one true mate. She was his everything. Finally, finally, she was his. He kissed her back with the fervor of the Hunga Tonga–Hunga Haʻapai underwater volcano eruption. His heart was exploding, his dragon pushed to rise up. It was demanding he mark her, claim her, and mate her.

"Get a room, you two," someone nearby shouted at them. "Hey, this is a family event. Take that into your own home for Christ's sake."

"Orgasms, bro. Mates like lots and lots of orgasms." That last one came from the wizened warrior running the schmoonshine booth. But when Taika went to tell the guy that he knew what to do with his mate, he wasn't there. A wide-eyed, wrinkly, grandmotherly-looking woman stared back at him.

Lena broke the kiss way before he was ready. But she cupped his cheeks and stared deep into his eyes. "I do not entirely understand what's going on. I think that ice cream did something to me. I feel as though a darkness has been lifted from all around me."

"Same. Like a spell has been broken that's been keeping us apart." One that he had the feeling the White Witch had helped him break.

"Yes. Is that a thing? It must be." Her eyes flicked up and around, her brain accessing some kind of information or memories. "I feel so incredibly different. But one thing I do know is that one tiny shot of schmoonshine did not intoxicate me. I am fully aware of what I'm doing, and I just want to check that you are too."

"I have never been drunk in my entire life, chook." Liquor simply couldn't keep up with Dragon metabolism. He wouldn't want to be under the influence of anything but her anyway.

"But I want to tell you right now while we're both clear headed. I'm taking you home to have a lot of really dirty sex with you. So, if that's not what you're up for, say so now and we'll put the brakes on."

Was Lena checking in to make sure he was enthusiastically consenting to sex with her? She stayed silent, her eyes not leaving his for a moment. She was. If he wasn't a fully powered up Dragon Warrior, his knees might have gone a little bit weak for her.

"I very much want to go home with you and have all the really dirty sex. All of it. With you and only you. I want you so keenly that I would perhaps cause a full-on scandal in your small town to have you on my cock in the next sixty seconds, if that's what you also want."

She nodded and leaned in for another kiss, saying the only words he wanted to hear against his lips. "Yes, yes, and definitely yes."

She so very sweetly sought his consent to get down and dirty, but he didn't think she knew what she was getting into with him. They were mates. That was a forever thing. Not a one-night stand. It was a huge part of the instant attraction and, at least on his part, the insta-love he felt for her.

He expected all of this.

She didn't. That wasn't informed consent by any means. He'd had plenty of partners over the years who didn't know his true nature. But none of them were his fated mate. None were the one person he would both live and die for.

Lena was human and knew absolutely nothing about the supernatural world. He didn't understand how she wasn't freaked out by recognizing him as something more than human. As much as he wanted to absolutely ravage and rail her into a blissful oblivion of multiple orgasms, they had to talk. That wasn't going to be easy.

"Even though, I'm..." he glanced around to see who else might be listening, "a dragon?"

How did she even know? Must be in her genes.

"Well, I was today years old when I found out dragons are real and that they look a whole lot like humans. But I think it might be the absolute coolest thing that has ever happened in my entire life, and I'd really, really like to see what kind of naughty business we might get up to with your tail and my mouth, or other fun places. So, also yes. I want almost exactly that. But in the privacy of my house, which is about two blocks from here."

Kaboom. His head just exploded. "Which way?"

He didn't even bother setting her down. He walked straight out of that horrid rhubarb extravaganza and toward her home. He didn't even need her directions. Taika could find his way like there were runway lights and neon arrows pointing him in the right direction.

He wouldn't mark her until they could talk more about what it meant to be a Dragon's one true mate, but that didn't mean he couldn't do all the other fun things they both wanted to do tonight. Apparently involving his tail.

It only took him a minute to get them to her house, and when he was prepared to kick open the front door and fix her locks and door jamb later, a big gust of wind came along and blew it open for him. Huh. He peeked at Lena to see if she knew what she'd done, or if being a wind witch was also news to her.

She had a surprised mouse face. "Did you do that with your dragony superpowers? Do dragons have superpowers?"

Taika didn't stop to answer her question, he kept going right into her house, straight down the short hallway, and into her bedroom. He laid her down into the cushions and crawled over her, caging each and every one of her soft curves under his body. "We do, and my particular talent is in getting you all wet."

Lena threw her head back and laughed in a way that was so sexy and delicious it rumbled around his chest and made its way straight down to his cock. This was going to be the best kind of sex. Love and laughter.

"Don't believe me?" To prove his point, he breathed out a stream of water that he formed into a dragon that swam around their heads.

"Oooh. Fancy." She held her fingers up, letting the water glide over the tips. He could feel her touching his element just as if she was caressing him.

He curled the water dragon around her hand and arm and watched as her eyes danced with the wonder and magic of it all. He couldn't wait to get her into the ocean and introduce her to his Wyr, and then maybe some merpeople.

"I'm sure a skill in making mystical beasts out of water comes in very useful." She waggled her eyebrows at him, and he was dying to mark and claim her so he could hear each and every one of those dirty thoughts she had running through her mind right now.

"It does, and after I've made you come at least a dozen or so times, I'll take you somewhere we can play in my element." The thought of seeing her naked and wet had his cock and his dragon up and paying attention.

She laughed again and he could just eat her up. In fact, he was going to do just that. "A dozen? I like a man with ambition."

"You doubt my prowess, chook?" He'd had a lot of sexual adventures in his life. Dragons were an eternally horny lot. He'd pleasured and taken pleasure in plenty of cocks and more cunts than he could count, thinking it had all been just fun and games. Until tonight. Now he realized it had all been simply practice so that he was the best kind of lover. The one that she deserved.

"I will be happy to prove it to you." He swirled his elemental water dragon across her shirt and literally washed her top away. Then he did the same to her skirt, until all that was left was her adorable yet sexy matching bra and panties. It didn't hurt one bit that they were both a deep, dark shade of blue with a lighter blue design on them.

His dragon liked that very much and wanted to covet those undergarments and keep them in his hoard as a treasure. The horny ass human side of him wanted them gone. Right the fuck now.

He slid his hand up her inner thigh and carefully shifted one talon. He slit the fabric right across the waist-band and then again over her plump mound. Then he grabbed the shredded panties and slid them right out between her legs, dragging them along her sweet cunt.

"Hey," she giggled as he dangled them in front of her. "Those were my favorite Fri-yay undies."

He tossed them over his shoulder and pushed her knees open to expose her thick pussy lips and that luscious cunt. "Do you have multiple pairs of Fri-yay undies?"

"No." She gasped as he dipped his head between her legs and licked a circle all the way around her clit. Her next words were more of a whimper. "Thus, why they were my favorite."

"Then I'm not the least bit sorry about that." He spread her legs even wider and teased her by licking up one side of her clit and down the other. "I would happily destroy every pair you own, Fri-yay, or not."

She grabbed his head, threading her fingers into his hair, and ground her cunt against his lips. She wanted more and he was going to give it to her. "I'd let you if you keep doing that. Oh, gawd, yes. Right there. Ooh, a little to the left."

Fuck yeah, how he loved a partner who wasn't afraid to tell him what and how they needed him. She thought a dozen orgasms was going to be a challenge? Not with the communication and the chemistry they had. He licked and sucked her clit until she was nice and wet and whimpering with need.

While he very much wanted to taste her as she came in his mouth, he wanted to see her face as he gave her this first climax. Seeing how he could drive her to the brink would be almost as good as getting to mark and claim her.

He pushed two fingers inside and gave her one last suck before he bobbed his head up and kissed his way up her rounded belly and across the soft material of her blue bra.

"Oh, no. Don't stop. Please. I'm so close."

Her whimpers were so delicious he wanted to eat them up too. "I know, chook. I'll take you there, I promise. I want you looking deep into my eyes when you come. I want to see every second of the pleasure I'm giving you."

He slid his fingers in and out, opening her for him and searching for the right spot to make her go crazy. She arched her back and cried out. Yep. There it was. "Did I mention I'm really good at finding things, like say, g-spots?"

"Holy crow, yes, yes you are." She clasped his arm in her hands. "More."

Goddess, she was beautiful, all worked up, flushed, and utterly feminine. Taika moved his thumb up so he could rub it back and forth over her clit with each thrust of his fingers. Lena threw her head back, exposing her throat to him and his mouth watered so much he had to lick his lips and swallow three times to keep himself from diving in and marking that luscious skin calling to him.

"Look at me, Lena. I want your eyes locked to mine when you come." His dragon reared up inside, on the verge of taking over just so he would mark her. It was almost unbearable seeing her creamy skin bare where the symbol of his dragon should be.

She blinked up at him, her breath coming in short, fast sucks of air. "Taika, I need... something more. I don't know what, but I need more of you."

Dammit. He knew her body craved his mark, his claim. He wouldn't do it until she understood what it meant, but he could give them both a taste. "I know what you need."

He pressed a kiss to her jaw and nibbled his way down to her ear and scraped his teeth across the little gold chain she wore and down the tight muscles in her neck. The taste of gold rushed his taste buds and went to his head like the most potent of schmoonshines.

"Jumping jellybeans, that is it. Do that again, and again, and more. I need more. I need you, Tai." Her words went straight to his heart, or maybe his soul, and his dragon could no longer be contained.

He'd made a huge mistake thinking he could do anything less than take her as his dragon demanded.

Mark.

Claim.

Mate.

Mine. Mine. She is mine.

His dragon fangs burst into his mouth and his vision went pure blue. His soul shard lit up her skin, her room, their very world. He thrust his fingers in exactly the way she needed, seeing and sensing every emotion, want, need, and desire like his own roadmap to her soul. He growled, warring with himself, trying to hold back, but he lost the battle with his base animalistic instincts and sunk his teeth into the one spot that would forever wear the mark of his dragon.

Lena threw her arms around his neck and cried out his name, coming so hard he could feel the pulse of her clit and channel spasming under his touch. "Taika, ooh god, yes. Taika."

"Lena, you're so fucking perfect, I can't believe your mine." The words were meant to be only a thought, but his dragon pushed it out into the mindspeak especially between mates.

She was still riding the waves of her orgasm and her response was both the cutest and the sexiest thing ever. *"I never knew orgasms came in colors, but my new favorite color is blue, definitely blue."*

MAKE ME YOURS

Why had no one ever told her about dragons and how good they were in bed? She and Taika hadn't even done the actual do yet and she was already flying high on one of the best orgasms she'd ever had. Ever. Like not even the best she'd ever gotten from a guy. The. Best. Ever.

And he thought she was going to have eleven more tonight? Yeah, uh, only if she was going to die from an oxytocin hormone overdose. Way better than all the people who OD'd on oxycontin. Way better.

When she had recovered and could breathe and open her eyes, the room was still bathed in the blue light from his necklace. "Why does the charm you wear glow like that?"

Taika stared down at her neck, and there was some self-recrimination in his gaze. She wondered if he'd given her a hickey or some kind of bruise when he'd bitten her.

She touched his cheek and rubbed her thumb over his bottom lip. "Hey, I loved every second of what we just did if you couldn't tell, and I'm counting on rounds two, three, four, etcetera to be just as fun. I told you I wanted to do all the dirty things with you."

He swallowed a bit harder than she liked but nodded. "This is my soul shard, a gift from my creator that contains a bit of his soul and mine. It gives me the ability to shift into a dragon, and it lights up only when I'm in the presence of my one, true, fated mate."

"Me?" It was almost as if he was speaking this whole other language and yet somehow, she understood every single word.

"You." His eyes twinkled when he said that, but there was a deeper worry inside of him that she wanted to soothe. "Maybe we need to talk about me being a Dragon Warrior and you being... you before we keep going."

He was being profoundly serious, and Lena just... couldn't be. Everything about how they'd met was strange and weird, and she was sure most women would see a thousand red flags, but she trusted Taika. He'd been a good guy from the first moment, and she refused to believe any less of him now.

Was it super bizzarro that he was quite literally a creature from books and mythology? Yep. Was that fucking badass? Uh-huh, sure was. That she was getting a chance to be involved with such an interesting and unknown part of the universe was so much more than she could have ever expected out of life. "I'm down for snacks, snuggles, and secrets. That's half the fun of intimacy with someone new, for me. The getting to know each other's bodies and minds."

"Why couldn't I have met you before the final battle with Hell?" He shook his head but his whole body relaxed. "I can't believe my soul shard didn't direct me to you the last time I was in the States."

"Oh, we are definitely going to need snacks for this. Battle with Hell? Awesome." She jumped up, finally slipped off her bra, which she threw in Taika's face, and yanked the lightweight blanket off the bed to wrap around herself on her trek to the kitchen for late night sustenance. "Wait. Can you use your water trick to grab the ice cream out of the freezer, or is that too much?"

"It's not normally how I use my power over the element, but I can. Why don't you try with your power over the wind?"

What? Like... what? She flopped back onto the bed and looked him straight in the face. "Say more words."

He looked like a cat who'd caught the canary. She'd be his canary every time. "You, my sweet chook, are an elemental witch. You have power over wind. I've seen you use it several times."

Lena jumped right back up off that bed and started dancing around the room. Well, more jumping up and down like a little kid who just got five dollars to take to the one-penny candy store, and less actual dancing. "I'm a witch, I'm a witch. I am a freaking witch."

There had always been rumors that the Walker sisters,

her great, great aunties, had been witches. Not the horrible kind that ate children, but the good kind that respected nature and used their powers for good. The aunties had fed a lot of hungry people back in their day and were a proud part of Walker Valley heritage. Now she knew at least some of the stories were true.

Which also meant her mama wasn't as crazy as she'd thought.

When she had her dancing out of her system, she jumped back onto the bed, laid the biggest, hottest kiss on him, and then hugged him tight. "Show me how."

When she let go, he had a bit of a dumbfounded look on his face. He gave himself a shake, kind of like a wet dog. "First of all, we are doing more naked dancing later." He spun his finger at the floor where she'd been jumping around, and his eyes glazed over again for a second.

She snapped her fingers, and he came back to her.

"And second, my element is water, not wind, so any instruction I gave you would be just a little south of correct. But you have more control over it than you realize already. You're the one who opened the front door, and I'm not sure how it worked, but you use both the wind and some kind of affinity for gold to get all those people to fork over some cash when you sing."

Oh. Ohh. That was remarkably interesting. "So, you're saying if I decided to walk myself into Nashville and start up a singing career like Dolly Parton, that I'd make a lot of money?"

Taika shrugged. "I don't know who Dolly Parton is, but if she's a rich singer, then, probably."

Lena froze right where she sat and her jaw dropped open so wide of its own accord, she was gonna catch flies. "What do you mean you don't know who Dolly Parton is? Who do you think I've been dressing up as all this time? Whose songs do you think I've been singing?"

He made an oops smirk because he knew he was in trouble. "Aren't they your songs?"

"No, no they are not." She could hardly hold back her what-rock-have-you-been-living-under laugh. "That is something we will remedy with a Netflix and chill session later. You do know what that means, don't you?"

"I'm a dragon, not dumb. But trust me, you won't need Netflix to chill with me, chook." He reached for her, but she blocked his handy hands with a karate block she learned from the movies.

"Hold that thought, please. Can we circle back to the part about me learning how to use magic witchy powers?"

"One of the women you met at the diner, Ciara, is a white witch. She has power over the four earthly elements. And there's a whole slew of Gold Dragon Warriors and a few of their mates here too that I'm sure could help."

"Wait. Everyone who is here for your family reunion is a dragon or a witch, aren't they?" Duh. Of course, they were. There had definitely been something wrong with her. Between the time that she met Taika that first night and when she'd eaten the ice cream, was like a fuzzy dark dream.

"Yes to who and what they are. We aren't here for a family reunion though. It'll be easier to explain if I just take you to see them."

"Okay. Let's go." She moved to get off the bed again, but this time Taika grabbed her into his arms, trapping her in the most delicious way.

He nuzzled her neck in the spot he'd bitten, sending all kinds of tingles up and down her body. "Right now?"

Oh. No. Definitely not right now. There were particularly important other things to do right here in this bed. Like finally get him undressed so she could taste each and every one of those a hundred and sixty-six pack abs. "First, I want you to fuck the daylights out of me, then I want to do the same to you, and then once more for funsies. Then we'll go meet your family and see what kind of shenanigans you lot are getting up to in my Smokey Mountain home."

She reached for his shirt and worked her way down the buttons. He started from the bottom, and it didn't take more than a few seconds for her to get the ab-a-liscious wish.

"This is a plan I can get behind." He stripped off the shirt and, my oh my, did he have great shoulders. She was going to spoon the hell out of him later. "But we didn't talk about being a dragon's mate. I don't want you thinking I dragged you into this without understanding what it all means."

"Tell me and fuck me at the same time." She was already on to his pants. How was she completely naked and he wasn't? That was crap. Ooh. Was this a suitable time for elemental wind magic? Taika had used water magic to undress her.

She closed her eyes and thought ridiculously hard about what she wanted to happen. There was a whooshing sound, and something was definitely happening. When she opened her eyes, Taika's hair was flying around like he was in one of those hurricane machines and he was squinting to try and keep the wind out of his eyes.

"Oops. Sorry. Just thought I'd try to whip your pants off with my super-duper magic powers." She flicked her hand toward his waist and all of a sudden, a very different gust of wind whirred through the room, and poof, Taika's pants were draped over her bedside lamp. And the man wasn't wearing any underpants.

Because, you know, he probably didn't have any extra room in his trousers for even a scrap of fabric. That was a whole hell of a lot of man he was carrying around between his legs.

Taika folded his arms all smug-like. "Chook. You're staring."

"Well, yeah." She waved her hand in the direction of his very large, very erect penis. "Wouldn't you if you'd just imagined trying to fit something the size of an entire Naval Destroyer in your whoo-ha?"

"Oh, trust me, love. It will fit."

"I'm game to find out if you are."

"Sounds like the best kind of game to me. But I think you're playing another one that lets us avoid talking about you being my fated mate."

"If that means we're destined to be together, and we're going to do stuff right here, right now that will seal that deal, I'm not sure what makes you think I'm not one-hundred and sixty-nine percent on board for that."

"You know nothing of Dragon culture, history, or—" Lena put her finger over his mouth, and he tried to keep talking so she stuck it in his mouth and forcibly held his tongue down.

He did very naughty and inappropriate things to her finger, but she persevered because he needed to know she both wanted him and accepted him for exactly who he was. "Stop right there. I don't need to know any of it, although I'm looking forward to learning all about you and your people, and my people for that matter."

She crawled into Taika's lap and didn't mind even a little bit that his cock was poking her in the leg. She only hoped she wasn't squishing it into not being usable in a few minutes. Even if it was, she needed to soothe his sweet soul that was so worried about her being okay with who he was.

"Sweet dragon of mine, do you think I want to go out on dates and hope that the other person likes me, or worse, doesn't find me repulsive? Because I've been on plenty of those. There are a lot of horrible humans in the world and most of them are on dating apps.

Knowing that all along there has been someone out there in the universe especially for me, and I'm the one and only for them, it's not only a relief, it's fan-fucking-tastic."

He pulled her fingers from his mouth and pressed a kiss to her palm. "You don't mind that fate has decided and we don't get a say in it?"

"It's god damned exhausting having to make every single decision in my life. Go to work and be subjected to creepy Billy or stay home and watch old Dolly Parton movies? Forcibly take my mama to a therapist or let her be, knowing she's getting worse? Try rhubarb schmoonshine or not? The answer to that one is not, by the way."

She pushed her hands into his hair and brushed her lips across his. "I'm elated that I don't have to do the work of finding someone I'm compatible with and might have feelings for, and I still get an amazing, sex on a stick, dragon to love for the rest of my life. We get to skip to the good part and if TikTok has taught me anything, that doesn't happen to most people."

Taika's smile lit up the whole room even brighter than his soul shard. Then he said, "Who is TikTok? Another country and western singer?"

Oh no. Dragon culture was really behind the times. "You're killing me, smalls."

He chucked her under the chin and snickered. "I'm just kidding, I know he's a rapper. And I assure you, I'm not small."

See? How could she not have fallen for him even

faster than she had? "No, no you're not. However, the question of fitting remains to be tested."

Something flashed in Taika's eyes, and for the first time, she recognized it as his dragon. He growled and she loved that he was done playing and now they were going to have the real fun.

He grabbed her around the waist and flipped her around, pressing her down into the blankets and pillows. "Ass up, my sweet mate. I'm about to teach you all about how Dragon Warriors claim their mates."

Doggy style had never been her favorite position, but she had a feeling dragon style would be a whole lot better. She propped her knees underneath her and shook her bottom at him. Taika gave her butt a little smack, not enough to hurt, but just enough to wake up all her senses. Which she was going to need, because she didn't want to miss a single moment of this claiming he mentioned.

"Fuck, your cunt is so wet for me." He notched his cock right at her entrance and whoo, there was no way he was getting even the tip in. No. Way.

He grabbed a hold of her hips and pushed forward so slowly, she was sure she was going to lose her mind. Because not only did he fit, he filled her up in a way no one ever had before. Having him fit the two of them together like they were one was so much more pleasure and emotion than she expected. "More, Taika. Take me, make me yours."

He growled again and thrust in deeper and deeper until she couldn't take anymore. Then he pressed one hand against her back, making her arch, and he pushed further with one hard thrust. "That's right, good girl, take it all. Yes, you are mine, sweet Lena. Mine."

He withdrew, faster than he'd seated himself, and thrust back in, just as deep, and set up a rhythm, pistoning into her, his hips slapping against her bottom. With each push inside, he growled and said that she was his until there was only his voice and her building orgasm.

Just like before, she was so close to the edge, but she needed more of him. "Taika, more, I need you. I need more of you."

He shoved deep into her and held himself there, then leaned forward so his body completely covered hers. He wrapped his arms around her chest and lifted them both up, so they were on their knees and locked together. With a suave move, he pushed one hand between her legs to stroke her clit and lowered his mouth to that tingly spot on her neck.

Oh yes. This is exactly what she needed. Lena melted into him, letting him control her body and her pleasure. He took long thrusts and sank so deep inside of her that she shook with need as he withdrew.

The necklace she wore went berserk between her breasts, and Taika grabbed the charm. The moment he touched it, it disintegrated into a thousand rainbow-colored sparkles. Somewhere deep in her soul, she understood that the necklace had kept her safe and had brought Taika to her. It was good and right that his touch replaced all the feelings of comfort and home it had represented to her.

He kissed her neck and whispered into her ear, "I give everything I have to you, my mate. You're mine and I am yours. Forever."

"Forever," she whispered back.

He groaned so very deeply, showing her his pleasure at her words. With one more long thrust, he sunk his fangs into her skin and together they both exploded into the most powerful climax, coming together, becoming one.

EVERYTHING AND MORE

Taika held Lena tight in his arms and buried his face into her soft hair. Now that the curse was broken, she smelled like vanilla, ripe peaches, and ice cream. He couldn't get enough of it. Nor could his dragon.

There was no way that he could have stayed away if he'd scented her from the beginning. Whoever had laid that curse on them, that blocked his senses, really knew what they were doing.

At some point he was going to have to investigate who was trying to keep him from finding his mate. There was definitely some kind of evil at work here and if it extended beyond him and Lena or this area, the Dragon Warriors would need to get involved.

Just because the war with Ereshkigal was over, didn't mean humans and dragons were safe from other dark forces. This was just the first time they'd experienced any tangible threat since the final battle with Hell, and that had him off kilter.

Lena snuggled into his chest and made an adorable little humming sound. He wasn't yet done giving her those dozen orgasms, but they'd worn each other out. She was a great fucking lover, always making sure he knew what would make her feel good and checking in with him to see what he wanted too.

There was nothing sexier than a lover with confidence in the bedroom. He'd been with plenty of people who didn't have that, and he thanked the fates he'd been matched with a woman who knew what she wanted and wasn't afraid to say so.

Her sleepy hums turned into an actual tune, but nothing he recognized. As she hummed her little ditty, sparkles of light flittered around above their heads like stars. She was literally singing up the sunshine. Her magic was fascinating in the ways it manifested, and yet she really didn't seem to have a clue that she was anything more than average.

It would be fun to see her learn what she could do. He was anxious to officially introduce her to the other mates, who would be able to teach her how to use her power over the elements in the way that they did. But later, much, much later. Like five more orgasms later.

He danced his fingers up and down her arm along to the tune and then across her lovely and large breasts. She squirmed under his touch, and he teased her nipples, wanting to wake her in the best possible state. One of arousal.

"I was having the best dream that a dragon was touching me in all the right places with some decidedly dragony appendages." She made an adorable humming sound and snuggled deeper into his chest.

"You have a preoccupation with my tail, don't you?" They would definitely be playing naughty games with his tail and her plump ass later. But when they had more room. Her house was... tiny. At least compared to the wide open spaces of New Zealand that he was used to.

"Yes." She ran her fingers over his jaw. "Yes, I do."

"I guess that's fair since I have a preoccupation with making you come." He rolled over so her body was beneath his and shifted only his tail, just to tease her. "I believe I owe you at least six more orgasms."

"Nope. No. No way. It is my turn." She rolled, pushing him onto his back and straddled him before he could even protest. Not like he would. "I've been wanting to do this since I got your pants off."

Lena scooted down and bent her head over his cock and then licked him from base to tip like a fucking ice cream cone. A full body tremor rippled through him, and his dragon rose up to the surface, wanting to mark her, claim her, and mate her all over again.

She teased his tip with her tongue. "Can I ask you something?"

He gritted his teeth and pushed his dragon and his

libido down. Because whatever she wanted was his priority. If she wanted to tease him and talk, that's what they would do. "Anything. Especially when you look at me like that."

She batted her dark lashes, gazing up at him through hooded eyes he could get lost in forever.

Lena licked her lips and dragged her teeth across her lips, a little shyly. "When we were in the restaurant, you said something about that your mate could be a she, he, or a they."

"Yep." He'd been worried for a minute she was going to ask him something hard. This he didn't mind talking about at all. "Gender has never mattered to me when it came to love, and certainly not sex. Ever since my first shift at puberty, I've been horny as shit. I'd fuck a plant if it felt good."

"Have you?" Her cheeks and chest flushed, and he knew exactly what she was thinking about.

"Fucked a plant?" He teased, because she was so adorably blushing. "No. But I have been with men, women, mermaids, mermen, and I tried it with a phoenix once. Fire and water is a steamy combination, but in the end, not right for either of us."

Her face turned thoughtful, and he wanted to make sure she was as comfortable with his sexuality as he was. He would tell her and show her anything she wanted. But none of it mattered. He may have been Pan, but he was Lena-sexual now. No one else in the world mattered to him or his cock. "Do my past conquests bother you?"

She smiled and wrapped her hands around the base of

his cock, slowly dragging her hand up and then down. "No. I think it's very sexy to be so filled with passion like that. But I'm not a disappointment to you, am I, because I'm just a plain human woman?"

First Dragon above. That's what this was about. He'd never considered she might worry about that. "Sweet Lena, no. I wanted love above all else, be that with a man or a woman or someone who is neither or both or in between. It's the feelings in my soul that mattered. Fate knew what was right for me. And that's you."

She stared down at him and bit her lip. "You're sure?"

He'd spend the entire rest of their lives proving to her that she was everything he ever wanted. "I knew it the second the curse was broken and I scented the real you for the first time. You're perfect exactly as you are."

Her eyes glistened and his heart skipped a beat or two. He'd never felt closer to anyone in his life and there never would be anyone else who held his heart and soul so securely. He'd told her with words, now he would show her with his body exactly how perfect they were for each other.

Taika cupped the back of her neck and pulled her in for a kiss. Before their lips even brushed, a scent so intense filled his mouth, nose, throat, and had his eyes watering like a thermal spring.

He jerked back and sneezed, once, twice, a half a dozen times.

"Oh no," Lena covered her mouth with her hands, "I thought we were past this."

Yes, they had broken the spell. But that meant whatever evil doer had cast it in the first place was here, in Lena's home. His dragon pushed at the surface, wanting out so he could seek and destroy. He would protect her from Hell itself if he had to.

But there was no room here to fully shift without destroying her house. Taika called upon the heightened senses of his beast and located the threat immediately. The little fucker was right outside the bedroom door. Once this threat was squashed, he'd be making sure her home had some supernatural security.

He put his fingers to his lips and gave a quick tilt of his forehead to indicate toward the door. She narrowed her eyes, quietly reached under the bed, and pulled out a baseball bat, gripping it tight and wielding it over her head. What he wouldn't give to see her with a sword.

She jerked her chin and carefully crept toward the door. Taika's instincts were to shove her behind him to keep her safe from any harm, but she'd likely knock his block off for it. His mate could take care of herself. But together, they would make a glorious team.

He rolled off the bed and nodded, asking her with his eyes if she was ready for him to open the door so she could clobber whoever was on the other side. If it was anything more than her bat could handle, he'd risk the structure of her house and shift to put himself between her and the danger.

Taika yanked the door open and was hit directly in the chest with an exploding vial of burning hot sauce. His dragon couldn't be contained at this affront and his beast burst into being. Mid-shift, the room exploded as his huge form broke down the walls and roof. His attack was met with a shot of spicy pain and suffering as his face was coated in a slurry of orange-colored peppery liquid tainted with dark magic.

"Billy? What the hell are you doing here?" Lena's angry shout and then the sound of her bat hitting something soft and fleshy, filtered through the shitstorm swallowing up Taika's vision and sense of smell. But this wasn't the same spell that had been cast on him before. It wasn't just eating away at his senses, he could feel something dark and ominous pulling, scratching, clawing at his very soul.

He whipped his tail around, searching for any target he could possibly take down with the sharp scales. With one hard swing, he took out another wall or two and maybe part of the ceiling. But while he put all of his might into the muscles, the world around him was fading into a black tunnel.

"Lena, run, go to the mountains and find the other dragons. They will protect you."

"I'm not leaving you, ever. So don't you even dare think about dying on me." He may not be able to see her or smell the acrid scent of dismay and anxiety on her, but the tremble in her voice gave away her fear for him.

No way was he letting death take him when he'd only just found his true mate. He reared up and spread his wings wide, ready to blind attack. Spikes of pain hit him directly in the chest, piercing through his scales. Whatever had hit him was there and gone in a flash. It hadn't penetrated deeply enough to cause real injury, yet far too rapidly he was being paralyzed, and that meant he couldn't protect his mate.

"Taika, look out!" Lena screamed at him, but the end of her shout was muffled. Someone or something was dragging her away and while he could tell she was putting up one hell of a fight, her cries came from farther and farther away.

With a final push of all he had inside his very soul, he used his greatest weapon of his element and spewed a stream of water and ice, hoping to both wash away the debilitating spell and hit his enemy. All that came out was a trickle of drool. What the fuck was in this dark magic?

He collapsed to the floor, having burned through the ends of his energy. The dragon part of him was now barely responding. This spell and the dark magic within were far more powerful than the one that had kept him from Lena in the first place.

"Lena, love, aroha, where are you?"

Even his mindspeak was barely more than a mere whisper. He couldn't even get it out of his own head to reach out to his mate.

Demon shite, someone was taking her and he couldn't do a damn thing. Even as he tried to jerk away at her warning and then drag himself to her, his muscles collapsed under him and he lost his dragon form. He shifted back to his weaker human flesh and collapsed on the bed they'd only just laid in claiming each other as mates.

He couldn't move, he couldn't think, and he was dying. His heart beat once, twice, and then no more. The darkness overtook him, and the last thing he saw was the flash of blue light before his soul shard extinguished.

RHUBARB AND OTHER DISASTERS

Lena mentally screamed at her muscles. She stood frozen, like a dumb deer in the headlights as Billy reached out and grabbed her arm, his cold fingers digging into her flesh. She struggled against his grasp, her pulse freaking out and her whole chest going cold. Her mind couldn't process what was happening, wouldn't believe it.

Billy had just taken out her mate and now he was trying to take her too. She had to fight back, but seeing him take her beautiful, amazing dragon down so easily, devastated her. He couldn't be dead. He couldn't.

She wrenched her body and arm, but Billy was too strong, his grip on her arm was like a vice. All she could think was that she had to get away, she had to get back to Taika. She twisted and writhed and pulled with all her strength, desperation giving her added power.

Billy sneered at her, his own strength somehow

bolstered by supernatural powers swirling around him like a dark cloud. He was enjoying this. Disgust and dread pooled in the back of her throat like bile bubbling up from the sick feeling in her stomach. He reveled in her fear and her struggle.

"You're coming with me," Billy hissed, his voice dripping each disgusting word out like black sludge. "You may be a powerful elemental witch, Lena, but you're no match for me and my... resources. Now quit fucking around with your disgusting attempt at bestiality and meet your new fate."

Lena was momentarily stunned by the hate in his eyes. What in the world had happened to him to make his soul go from douchebro to brimstone? Didn't matter, because he could fuck the fuck right off. How the hell did he know she had powers anyway?

She didn't know why he wanted her, but Lena was not going to let him take her away from her home and her mate. She had to fight. She had to survive. That woke her muscles up and she found the strength to pull away from Billy's grasp. She reached deep within herself and summoned every ounce of magical energy she had, focusing it into a bright white ball of light in her mind. Now if she just knew how the hell to use the power inside to hurt him and get away.

"I'm not going anywhere with you." Her voice might be shaking but that didn't mean she wasn't determined to tell this asshat where he could shove his resources. "I don't know what you think you're doing. But if you think you can use me or my magic for your own selfish purposes, you can go screw yourself."

Billy sneered at her, his own magical powers swirling around him like a dark cloud. "You think you I want your powers? Pathetic." He spat on the ground at her feet. "You're nothing but a foolish backwoods girl."

She might be backwoods, but she was country girl strong. She closed her eyes and wind whipped around her, pushing Billy away.

The attack caught him off guard, and he staggered backwards, his own strength dissipating. Lena took her chance and fled, running as fast as she could back to the safety of her room. Which, oops, was not so much a room, but a disaster area. It looked like a tornado hit, but that had been her dragon trying to protect her.

Now Lena had to protect him if she could.

Before she made it into the doorway something wet and sticky hit her smack dab in the middle of her back. She didn't smell the distinct scent of hot sauce from before, but something bitter and fruity. Instantly her body grew heavy and her eyes drooped. Her vision tunneled, going dark around the edges, but less like she was fainting and more like she was falling asleep. What was this, a frickin' narcolepsy spell?

She tried to fight it, forcing her legs to take another step and another. She stumbled and only just managed to throw her arms out to catch herself before she hit the floor. So... tired. Her limbs wouldn't move, so with the last bit of consciousness she had she tried opening her mind to Taika.

"I won't stop fighting for you. But Billy has gotten the better of me. Please, Taika, be okay. Tell me you're okay."

There was no response. Darkness closed around her and the remaining strength she had melted away. She was now at Billy's mercy.

She slipped into unconsciousness, she could feel herself being lifted off the ground and carried away. She floated in a weird hazy darkness and either dreamed or hallucinated shadowy demon things that looked like a cross between bats, ostriches, and deformed weird dragons. Those had better be hallucinations anyway.

It was so weird because she was at the edge of awareness of what was happening to her and around her, but couldn't move or do anything about it. Billy took her someplace dark and damp and wasn't gentle setting her down. She was definitely going to have bruises.

Slowly, the darkness in her mind and body lifted, and when she awoke, she found herself in a dank cave, surrounded by strange, shadowy figures. Oh crappola. Was it the batstriches?

She tried to sit up, but her head was throbbing and she felt disoriented. She closed her eyes and took a deep breath, trying to clear her head.

When she opened her eyes again, there weren't any monsters, only piles of debris and another woman with her in the cave. If Billy was running some kind of supernatural woman trafficking operation, she really was going to shove his magic hot sauce where the sun don't shine.

"Where are we?" Lena asked, her voice weak and reedy.

"You're safe for now," the woman with ultra-pale skin and stark black hair said soothingly. "That piece of trash brought you here, but I won't let him hurt you if I can help it."

Oh. She'd met this woman before. It was Jada from the group of women who'd been trying to find Taika a date at the restaurant.

Jada opened her mouth and flashed some sharp looking fangs for Lena. Whoa. Taika hadn't said anything about vampires. But if Billy had the ability to capture a freaking vampire lady who could eat him for lunch, he was into some serious dark shit.

"He's a bad man and a worse singer. What I don't understand is how he captured us. Do you remember what happened?"

"He's not like any supernatural I've come across before. He's gotten access to some dark magic, but it's not from my people or Ereshkigal, so I'm at a loss."

"I don't know who Air-ish-kuh-gal is. Is it a vampire like you?" A. She couldn't believe she'd just blurted that question out like being a vampire was a perfectly normal occurrence in her world, and B. Lena sure wished she and Taika had broken their spell earlier so he could have given her some more info about his world.

She refused to believe Taika was dead or that he

wouldn't be able to come for her. She would know if he'd died. She. Would. Know. And since she was sure he wasn't, she could stay calm and collected and pretend her world hadn't just gone from boring to paranormal in the span of a few hours.

She would believe he was coming for her. And when they were together again, they could find a way to defeat Billy and stop him from harming anyone else.

Like throwing him into a lake of his own stupid hot sauce. If she never ate or even smelled a Nashville hot chicken sandwich ever again, that would be fine by her.

"I'm a succubus, not a vampire, and Ereshkigal is—umm, are you all right?" Jada moved closer and stared at Lena. "Your face is going all blotchy."

Lena's head was spinning and her throat felt tight. She'd thought it was just after effects of Billy's narcolepsy spell, but nope. She touched her face and looked around frantically. There was only one thing her mother had told her she was allergic to her entire life.

It wasn't until she saw the clusters of pale green stalks growing in the corners of the cave that she realized the what the piles of debris were made of. "Shit on a stick. That's all rhubarb, isn't it?"

She had no idea how it had ended up in this cave, but she knew she had to get away from it as fast as possible. "I think I'm allergic to rhubarb. I gotta get out of here."

Wait. Was she allergic? Her mind was so muddled. She'd gone to the Rhubarb festival and been fine. Was this confusion part of Billy's spell?

The other woman looked at her with concern and quickly came to her side. “That doesn’t make sense. You’re a daughter of dragons. The human part of you should counter the Dragon side, just like it does in the rest of us. Have you ever had an allergic reaction to it before?”

“What?” This was why she’d never been to the rhubarb festival before. But she’d had the rhubarb schmoonshine and been fine. Oh, and that pie that ended up all over her the other day at the diner. No hives then.

Lena's head was spinning as she tried to process this information. Daughter of dragons. Daughter. Dragons. This is what her mother had been hiding from all these years. She just knew it.

All she wanted was the truth from her mother, to be able to live a real and authentic life. She'd clearly missed out on too much.

Jada pulled Lena to her feet and guided her to the area where slivers of light came through. “Rhubarb is the main ingredient in the pastries I've used in the past to fight the demon wyrms. It's a powerful plant, especially when it comes to defeating any demon wyrms. We could make a whole lot of incendiary desserts with all of this stock.”

Rhubarb hurt demons? What in the moonshine was going on here? “Maybe I’m just having a plain old panic attack. I sure could use some fresh air.”

Lena wanted to ask Jada about the whole dragon's daughter thing, but she had so many mixed emotions and a flurry of questions only her mother could answer flowing through her head like a damn tornado. She reached out and ran her fingers over a stalk of the rhubarb. How many lies had her mother told her over the years?

It only took a few breaths and some time to arrange all the pieces in her mind to understand that Lena was not the only one in the cave who was the fated mate of a dragon. Jada must also have a dragon mate.

That probably meant all the girls from the restaurant were too. And that all their husbands were dragons. This was so crazy. But it felt right. True. "Jada? Do you know what I am?"

"Yeah. It's hard for me not to see it. That light inside of you almost hurts my eyes." Jada raised her hands and made an embarrassed 'oh' with her mouth. "Sorry, not that it's bad. I'm just more of a nighttime half-demon, you know?"

She didn't know, but she wanted to learn. "Any chance you know how to teach me to use my power? Taika and I were messing around with it, but I just found out a hot minute ago that any of this," she swung her finger around indicating the whole world, "even existed, so I'm starting from the beginning."

"Not a clue, but I could show you how my power over my element works. I was about to open a shadow portal to try and escape, but then you arrived."

Eek. Lena hoped a shadow portal wasn't as bad as it sounded. "I'm game if you are."

Jada held up her hand, a ball of sparkling black fog

forming in her palm. She closed her eyes, focusing all her energy on opening the portal, and Lena could feel the air around them start to shimmer.

Suddenly, there was a loud, earsplitting noise, and a swirling portal opened, revealing a vortex of what looked like coal-black bubbling clouds. "Where does it go?"

"Wherever I want it to. Although, I have to warn you, I don't always get that right. So, it could be home, or it could be Hell."

Lena's heart went into running rabbit mode. This was their way out, but it was also one hell of a gamble. Oops. Pun not intended.

"Ready?" Jada was just about to step through but a horde of something so dark and malevolent formed at the apex of the portal. The cave went from dank to ice cold and Jada fell to her knees.

Lena gasped, her hands instinctively reaching out to catch Jada. "Close it, close it quick."

In the span of a blink the portal zipped shut and only the pale light from the doorway and the smell of rotting rhubarb remained.

"What in the Hell was that?" Pun intended that time.

"I... I don't know. I've never seen or felt anything like it before and I've been in and around Hell and demons my entire life. That... that was so much worse than anything Ereshkigal has at her disposal." Jada's voice shook, matching the tremors in her body.

"Okay. So let's not do that again. Scratch plan A."

"Yeah, but now we really have to get out of here. I've

got to warn Ky and Jett. If that's hiding in the shadow, the Black Dragons can't use their element. Crud. I hope my sister is okay."

Well, shit. They were even more trapped now than before, and she was no closer to learning how to use her own power to help them get out of there. This was no way to save herself or get back to Taika

ONLY MOSTLY DEAD

In the early morning light, Taika let his mind wander in the magical place between dreams and consciousness. For the first time in his life, his soul felt full. Too full even.

He'd marked and claimed his mate. There was only one thing left to do, and that was to give Lena his soul. He would have last night as they made love, but somehow, they always got caught up in the pleasure, and the right moment wasn't there.

That meant he had to find the right time, and his favorite thing in the world, next to hearing Lena cry his name when she came, was finding things. He knew just how to find this one too. He had the perfect resources at his fingertips. The Wyvern's mates. Ciara would be pee her pants excited to help him find the right time and place to have a mating ritual.

He tried to stretch and instead he sneezed. That's

when he realized something was wrong. He couldn't move and he couldn't fully wake up. He reached out to Lena via their new mindlink. *"Lena, love. Where are you, and are you okay?"*

He got no response. Fuck.

"Ky, are you there? Something has happened to my mate."

Nothing.

Double fuck.

He opened his mind one more time and decided to call out for any being that might be able to hear him. No, if he couldn't contact neither Lena nor Ky, something much worse was wrong. He needed a higher power, and he knew of only one that might be able to help him *"First Dragon, hear my cry."*

Now, Kur, my love. He's asking for our help, so don't be too hard on him. That was definitely not the First Dragon's voice. It was feminine and soothing, and motherly even.

We keep telling them the same thing. Mark, Claim, Mate, give her your soul. They aren't hard instructions, and still these douchepotatoes keep fucking it up. Then they want us to step in and fix it all for them.

Oh, shit. Now that was the First Dragon. It had to be.

Sweetheart. You do have to admit he got pretty far along that path. He did mark her, claim her, and he definitely mated her. Besides, you're the one who told him to give his mate lots and lots of orgasms. That was keeping the two of them terribly busy.

Yep. Now all he wanted to do was give Lena his soul. Why couldn't he do that? Why couldn't he move, or see, or even smell where he was? He really, really hated feeling helpless. He was the one who helped others and that meant he had to be strong for them. Taika wasn't weak. He was the fucking Second Wyvern of the Blue Dragon Warriors.

Because kid, you went and got yourself killed.

Killed? What the actual fuck? That couldn't be right. He'd know if he was dead. Dead Dragons don't think. They didn't have desires. All he wanted or needed was to get back to Lena and make sure she was safe.

The motherly voice tsked. *Don't be silly. He isn't dead.*

Oh. Phew. He liked this woman and all she had to say.

Her presence wrapped around him like a warm, but slightly spiky hug. *He's just mostly dead.*

He had only one four-letter response to that. What?

Her warmth turned cool like a mountain lake, and despite his circumstances, she let her power over the elements wash over him. *And we all know that mostly dead simply needs a good reason to live. Do you have a good reason, Taika Puru?*

Hadn't he heard this in a movie once about a princess who was also a bride? Yes. He had. True love. That's what he had to live for. True fucking love.

Atta boy. The First Dragon praised him and for a moment, Taika thought he could actually see the rainbow of scales that each of their colors came from. *When you get back into your body, don't fuck around. Find your mate and give her your soul immediately, if not sooner.*

The soft coolness of the White Witch's embrace

turned icy and almost painful. *Then you drown that poison and its gateway to Hell and get rid of that murderous little fucker who thinks he can harness Hell's power now that Ereshkigal doesn't guard the gates. I don't like anyone stealing souls. Especially my dragon's daughters', you hear me?*

Yeah, he didn't like the sound of that at all. It wasn't like he could say anything, but the First Dragon and his mate did seem to understand his thoughts even though he wasn't mindspeaking with them. This was one weird afterlife.

Yes. I understand.

Good. Now, Inanna, my luscious mate. Do you have any chocolate to make this pill go down easier?

Her angry icy feel dissipated and he was once again bathed in the comfort of the four earthly elements. Afraid not. I ate it all. I do love chocolate.

The First Dragon chuckled. *I know you do, love. Too bad. This is gonna hurt, kid.*

Okay, he could take it. Or at least he thought he could. Some kind of fangs with the venom of a thousand suns, sank into his very soul and if he could, he'd scream and probably die of the pain, if he wasn't already dead.

Then he woke up and sneezed.

Ouch. He gripped his side, and his hand came away with blood. He was back in Lena's bedroom, but it was barely recognizable. The walls were covered in his blood and blue scales. The bed was covered in that disgusting hot sauce. Shit.

The pungent scent was already filling up his nose and

making his eyes water. He had to get out of here, but he also needed to try to track Lena's trail. She was nowhere in the vicinity that he could sense and even when he reached out to her mind, he got nothing.

If his soul shard wasn't still shining bright and he didn't absolutely know that she was alive, he would be worried. One horrible lesson Dragon Warriors had learned in the war with Hell was that a mate could survive the death of their Dragon Warrior, but if a mate died, so did their dragon.

If he was alive, so was Lena.

"Ky?" Surely his connection with his Wyvern worked now that he was alive again.

"Taika. Thank the First Dragon. Where the fuck have you been?"

"I'm not entirely sure, but I've got a piss of a mess here. My mate is missing, and I fear kidnapped. I'm injured and was left for dead."

"Jada has been taken too. Can you make it to the playing fields? The Greens can triage you and then you can join me in the hunt."

Fuck. Jada? Whoever was behind this was toast. Really dumb, soon to be dead, toast. Not just because he and Ky would rip this little fucker's entrails out and eat them with some nice fava beans, but he clearly didn't know the power that the women he'd taken had. Jada was a succubus and the Summer Shadow.

He could only hope that wherever they'd been taken, they were together.

"My dragon can heal my wounds. I'll be back inside the wards so I can shift and be back as fast as I can."

Gratitude and a modicum of relief passed through their connection from Wyvern to Second. *"Good. There's no other I want by my side more as we find whoever did this and destroy them."*

Taika ran to the front door. He needed to get outside and to head toward the nearest forested area that the local witches had warded to hide the dragons during the trials. Too bad they hadn't also had those witches ward against predators.

"Don't you move another inch, you beast. What have you done with my Jolene?" Lena's mother was standing in the doorway wearing a dress with food stains down the front, mismatched slippers, and brandishing a curling iron in her hand.

"I haven't hurt Lena. In fact, I'm trying to find her so I can protect her. I love her."

She scowled at him, slowly bent at the knees, not taking her eyes off of him, and plugged the curling iron into the nearest wall socket. When the little red light turned on indicating it was hot, she poked it in his direction like a sword.

With a thought he could douse her makeshift weapon and render them both harmless, but Lena had mentioned something about her mother not ever leaving the house because of her mental illness, so for her to be here now had to mean something.

"Mrs. Walker, do you know something about what's

happened to your daughter?" He very carefully walked toward her with his hands up in a surrender pose. "I know you've got some special abilities that you've passed down to Lena. Can you help me find her?"

She narrowed her eyes at him and kept her weapon steady. "How would you know anything about me?"

"I don't." Only what Lena had told him about her fragile mental health, and that she loved her daughter very much. "But you know something about me. I remind you of your husband, remember?"

With each question he inched slowly closer to her. As he did so though, his wounds were not healing. He needed to get into his dragon form. Just how freaked out would Lena's mother be if he shifted, snatched her up, and flew her up into the mountains where a hundred or so other Dragon Warriors awaited?

"I know you're a dragon." She waved her curling iron at him again. "What I don't know is why you think I would trust you. Those vile black dragons killed my Chrysós."

Black dragons, huh? More than ever, Taika was convinced that Chrysós had been a Gold Dragon Warrior, and Mrs. Walker his life companion. If demon wyrms had found him here and attacked, he would have given his life to save the woman he loved and his child. "The kind that looks like a bat and an ostrich had a demon baby?"

"Yes." She shuddered. "Friends of yours?"

He was close enough now that he could grab the

curling iron, but what then? "No, they were our enemies and we have destroyed them and defeated their maker. Those demon wyrms will never bother you ever again. But whatever darkness is lurking here in the valley can."

Mrs. Walker blinked a few times and her eyes bounced around in the exact same way as Lena's did when she was thinking about something. "Ask me again."

Which question? Shit, this was a hard conversation to follow.

She shook her head and the curling iron at him. "Ask me again if I know anything about what's happened to my Jolene."

Okay. He wasn't sure why he had to ask and she couldn't simply tell him, but he'd do whatever he could to get the info out of her. "Mrs. Walker, do you know what's happened to her? Can you help me save her?"

"I can hear her on the wind. I hear her a singing." She closed her eyes and tipped her head to the side, hearing something he couldn't. Then she started humming a tune and sang a few words. "I am a seeker."

"Where? Where do you hear her?"

"She's in the darkness, under the rhubarb." She made a face like she'd eaten something disgusting. "I told her not to go near that stuff. It's poison."

He did not like the sound of that. Was she buried alive? No, she wouldn't be singing if she was. Mrs. Walker must also be able to sense the darkness that Taika had at the field and her home. He didn't scent any fear from her though. Perhaps she was a tougher cookie than any of them knew. "Where is the rhubarb?"

"On the mountain behind the diner."

That was close enough to the playing field that they could gather an entire battalion of Dragon Warriors to battle this darkness and find the girls. "Thank you, Mrs. Walker. You've made my job of rescuing your daughter a whole lot easier. Can you stay right here? I'll send someone to come be with you."

"Don't you treat me like some fragile little bunny. You're... you're taking me with you, you hear?" She scrunched up her hands into fists, but not to fight. Not fight him anyway. She had her own demons and at the moment, she was beating the shit out of them.

"Yes, ma'am."

Taika led her outside, gave her a smile meant to reassure her, and shifted into his great blue dragon, hoping she wouldn't freak out, and any nosy neighbors weren't up at such an early hour.

She didn't. "Well, I'll be damned. Blue always was Jolene's favorite color. You got a saddle or something for me to ride on?"

WALKER FAMILY WITCHCRAFT BUSINESS

Two things Lena now knew for sure. Rhubarb could suck it, and Dolly Parton songs were the greatest method of keeping her from not freaking out.

If she never saw another stalk or leaf of this vile plant ever again, she would die happy. Lord-almighty. She didn't want to die. But her odds were not looking great.

She and Jada huddled together as far away from the bundles of rhubarb surrounding them as possible in this cold underground lair, or whatever it was. They leaned on each other more to have a connection to another person, and less to keep warm. Turned out that a succubus didn't have a whole lot of body heat to share. But her knowledge about having a Dragon Warrior for a mate, and singing, was what kept Lena going.

Jada squeezed Lena's hand. "Don't sing anymore sad ones, Lena. They aren't dead. We would know."

It was the four-hundred and seventeenth time she'd

said that same thing. It wasn't quite as comforting as the first few. "I'm about out of songs anyway, and I'm sure you're right."

That wasn't a lie. She did really believe that she would somehow know if Taika had died. She refused to believe Billy, what her eyes, or her memories said. He wasn't dead. Maybe just mostly dead, and that meant he was at least slightly alive.

Even if he was still alive, she absolutely knew he was gravely injured. Which meant he wasn't coming to rescue her. She and Jada had to rescue themselves.

"But we'll know for sure if we can find a way out of here." Nothing they'd tried so far had done a damn thing and she was beyond mad and frustrated. If and when she did get out of here, she was going to murder, kill, and maim Billy. In that order. And then in reverse order. And then do it all again.

"Okay. You're right. If I can't use my shadow—" Jada shivered. She'd tried that, and a really dark presence had tried to come through. "You're going to have to try your power over the wind element."

Singing to open peoples' wallets and whipping clothes off with a gust of wind didn't seem like it was going to be immensely helpful. Unless she had someone to whip the clothes off or to sing to.

Speak of the devil. A sliver of light shone at one end of the dirt cave. Billy's face popped through the crack of the door opening and he looked like he'd eaten shit on a shingle for breakfast. Guess working with the forces of evil wasn't treating him great.

Lena and Jada jumped to their feet and Lena concentrated on bringing a tornado down on Billy's head. Wind did whip around the room, but more like a light breeze that had potential to become, at best, a dust devil. She was ready to send a load of rhubarb leaves into his face instead, when he yanked the door all the way open and shoved another woman into the room. She stumbled and fell to one knee.

"Get on over there with the other two, you witch whore." Billy sneered and spit on the floor.

The woman slowly got to her feet and held one single middle finger aloft at him, but she didn't say a word. Her other hand was over her very large, rounded belly.

Oh no. Oh, God. It was Dixie Sue.

Despite the burn of the rhubarb gauntlet she had to push through, Lena rushed over and grabbed her friend and cousin into her arms. "Dix, are you okay? Of course not. Come here. I've got you."

Billy slammed the door shut on them and the room fell into darkness again. Shit. She hoped Dixie Sue didn't have as much of a burning allergic reaction to rhubarb as she and Jada did. Because getting back to the only corner of the cave with enough room to sit, was to go back through all those stacks of that crappy plant.

Dixie Sue gave a soul deep sad sigh, but then lifted her hand and snapped her fingers. A small flame lit on the nearest pile, then another down the path, and another, and another, forming a row of tiny lights like on an airplane aisle at night.

"Wow, Dix. I didn't know you could do magic like that." Lena looked over and in the dim light, saw the streaks of tears down Dixie Sue's face, and a grief-stricken haunting in her eyes. "What did Billy do?"

Dixie Sue shook her head and swallowed. Whatever it was, she wasn't ready to say it out loud.

"Okay. It's okay. Well, it's not, but we're together, and relatively safe for the moment, and we're going to plot various and sundry horrible revenges on Billy, so that's something." She led Dixie Sue to where Jada was and the three of them sat together, holding on to each other quietly for a long time.

Jada pulled away for just a moment and rustled around in her pockets. "I know it's not much, but it will help. I promise."

She held out a half of what looked like a Coal Miner's Daughter's donut, wrapped in parchment paper. "I'm sort of addicted to them, and I've been working on recreating the recipe for my bakery back home in New Zealand. There's some, umm, special ingredients in there that will make you feel better."

Dixie Sue stared at the half a donut, took it, and shoved a bite into her mouth. Her tears flowed down her face as she chewed, but by the time she swallowed, they'd dried up.

"He's a monster." The words came out of Dixie Sue's

mouth so quietly that if they weren't already in complete silence, no one could have heard them.

"I know," Lena said and held on tighter. "We're going to be monster murderesses."

Dixie Sue set her chin and nodded. "By being the witches Billy hates so much he would make a deal with a demon to get rid of."

Yeah. Girl power. But... "I'm pretty new to this witch business, Dix. I just discovered my powers a few hours ago, and to be honest, they're cool, but kind of weak. I can do a parlor trick, but that's about it. You saw my best effort just now and I'll I did was get a little dust in Billy's eye."

Jada looked at her funny. "You're a wind witch and the daughter of a dragon. That makes you doubly powerful. Plus, mate to a powerful Dragon Warrior. There's more than parlor tricks in you."

A swirling heat skittered up Lena's spine. "I'm an, excuse me, what?"

Taika revealed the witch business to her, but was Jada saying Lena's father was a dragon too? Ooh, she and mama were having a long talk later. "Dix, tell me I'm not the only one who didn't know about this."

Dixie Sue nodded. "You are. Sorry. Your mama just... Well, when your daddy got killed, she forbid everyone from telling you about the magic that runs in our family and your heritage. She didn't want anything to do with magic or other supernatural beings anymore. No one blamed her."

"So basically, Walker Valley is a giant haven for magic folk and mythical creatures and I'm the only one who didn't know? I suppose you're married to an Orc or something." No wonder she'd always felt out of place and stuck. All she ever wanted to do was get out of Sevier County and see the rest of the world. Because the rest of the world wasn't keeping secrets from her.

"No, Arthur is a bear shifter. Was. Arthur was a bear shifter. I don't know what he is now." The tears formed on her eyelashes again, but she blinked them away. "He's just an empty husk of a man. Alive, but there's nothing inside of him. We didn't even see what attacked him. But it's like his soul was stolen or something."

Crud. Her cousin had just suffered a horrible trauma and here she was complaining that she didn't know about her superpowers. "I'm sorry, Dix. I'm just frustrated that I didn't know. I feel like I could have done something to protect us all if I'd been allowed to see who I really am."

"Oh, you've been denying that all on your own. It's clear as day to everyone else that you're extra special, but you're the only one keeping yourself down."

Ouch. "Mama needs–"

"Oh, come on, Jolene. Your mama is blood related to half the town. You really think you're the only one who can help her out?"

Dixie bit her lip like she was trying to keep more words from coming out. It didn't work. "You're gonna hate me for saying this, but if we're letting everything out, you've been enabling her, and if you would have done the things you wanted to, like traveling the world or going to Nashville to be a star like we all already know you are, she might have had to work on herself and get better. But you baby her and then are resentful of it."

Double, triple, quadruple ouch.

Jada raised her hand and the two cousins looked at her. "I know what it's like to be in a family who has toxic secrets they keep and do stuff that they think is to help and keep their loved ones safe but is actually really harmful. Finding your way out of that kind of environment tends to help you realize you're a whole lot stronger than you ever knew."

Things Lena did not have on her bingo card for today were... too many to list. But finding out her daddy was a dragon, that her whole family were witches and knew that she was doing her mama more harm than good, and being told by a succubus that she needed to cowboy up, were at the top of the list.

"Okay. Umm. I hear you and I think my heart is a little bit broken. But if we can figure out a way to get out of here, I will talk to my mate and see if he can help me work on some of that." She really, really hoped that's what she would be able to do. She'd become a whole new person as long as it was with Taika. Although somehow, she knew she wouldn't have to for him. She did want to be a better person. Not just for her family, but for herself too.

"'Bout damn time." Dixie Sue pulled her into a hug. "Now, it seems all three of us are witches, that's good.

Power of three and all that. We should be able to combine our powers and multiply that to get us the hell out of here so we can take Billy down. That little fucker."

"But what do you get when you combine fire and wind? I think that's a forest fire and that won't be good trapped inside this cave or whatever it is." Lena was trying to think outside of the box, but it was hard when she was literally stuck in a box.

Dix looked over at Jada. "What's your elemental magic? I can't quite see it in you."

"Shadow," Jada said. "But we've already tried opening the shadow and some real bad soul stuff came after us. It's also keeping us from mindspeaking with our mates. So, I think I'm out."

Dixie rubbed her belly, head down, thinking. "My line of red witches has a thread of magic in us that has to do with the soul, and it's strongest when we're young, which I think is why Billy couldn't... do to us what he did to Arthur. I think the baby here protected us."

Lena started drawing these threads of information together in her mind. "My wind magic stuff isn't very powerful, but Taika said I was also using it when I sing, which I think means that's how I best know how to use it. I have an idea, and it's not without risks, but let me know if you think this will work."

She explained her plan of using Jada's shadow, which could serve like a sort of magical tunnel as far as she understood it, using Dixie Sue's special magic to keep the terrible things away, and her singing to call out to the witches and dragons and anyone else who might hear her to ask for help.

Dixie shook her head. "Even if I can get the baby to do something well beyond her comprehension at the moment, what if the only one who hears us is Billy?"

Those were all valid worries, and nobody had an answer. Jada pulled another half of a donut out of who knows where and took a bite. She nodded her head, and Lena didn't know if it was because the food was yummy or if she had an idea.

"You said Billy made a deal with a demon for this ability to break people's souls or whatever it is he's doing?"

"Yes." Dixie Sue's face went green. "I heard him talking to it. That's some dark shit he's dabbling in."

"I happen to have some connections in the demon world, ahem, since I am half demon myself, and my sister is Queen of the Succubus Court. What if instead of calling for help to get someone to come and rescue us, we sing up my sister instead, and see if she can't get Billy's demon to, you know, eat his face off?" She took another bite of her donut and this time, she had some sharp-looking fangs.

Dixie took one look at those fangs and rubbed her hands together with glee. "Even better."

Yikes. Lena better get her voice warmed up if she was singing a song to summon a demon from hell.

CURSES, GAUNTLETS, AND TRUE LOVE

Taika had been right about Lena's heritage. Turned out her whole mother's side of the family were witches, and her father had indeed been a Gold Dragon Warrior. Cage confirmed they'd lost one of his Wyr in this area twenty some odd years ago to a demon dragon attack.

"Why didn't I see what trouble that boy was?" Mrs. Walker grumbled. She'd turned into quite the little pistol since getting out of her house. She'd organized for the whole family to come up and help in the search. "I just wanted Jolene to find a nice normal human boy to fall in love with."

Humans could be just as much of monsters as the actual monsters.

She looked up at Taika and gingerly patted him on the arm. "You'll take care of my baby, won't you, so I don't have to put a spell on you?"

More of the Walker family that had helped ward the playing field, gathered along with the Dragon Warriors and they were as ready to go to war as Ky and Taika were. The local feud turned out to be a bigger deal than a couple of witches going catatonic.

Mrs. Walker was having the time of her life watching the rest of her family get all riled up on her and Jolene's behalf. "That Billy Whitecap and his ilk have always been trouble. Trying to mete out their own vigilante justice on folks who are just trying to live their lives. We need to teach him a lesson in manners."

Taika was itching to get riled with them and go find his mate, but this dark presence was keeping him and all the Blue Dragons from being able to use their finding sense. The best clue they had was still the singing that Lena's mum could hear, but that only gave them a general area where the rhubarb grew on the side of the mountain.

And the singing had stopped.

That freaked the piss out of Taika, but Ky continued to remind him if their mates were dead, they would know.

"I can't take much more of this standing around doing nothing. We have to do something to find the girls." Taika paced over the circle that Ky had already worn in the grass. All of the Wyverns and Seconds were using every bit of their ability, senses, and power over the elements to search for not just Jada and Lena, but several Walker witches who'd gone missing too.

The more Walkers that joined, the more information they gathered. Turned out they'd been hearing stories of witches from all across the country going missing, but because there was no specific governing body for all witches, no one had put together that the cases might be connected.

Whatever evil that Billy the shithead had accessed was far more powerful than demon dragons, that was for sure. If they were lucky, Billy would get himself killed. Although, then Taika couldn't torture him. Sure, sure, it would be under the guise of getting information, but really, he simply wanted to cut Billy's balls off and feed them to him for even thinking he could ever touch Taika's mate.

"I think I've got something here." Ciara and one of the Walker witches had their heads together over a sample of the vile hot sauce that had been all over Lena's bed. The two had used their combined powers to pull the elements out of the goo and had the separate ingredients floating over their heads.

Left on the makeshift stump table they'd been working on was a single downy barb of a black feather.

"Is that from a raven's feather? That's not our kinda magic. That is one powerful spell," someone from the family said.

"I can't tell what it is but watch this." Ciara combined her wind, sun, water, fire, and earth magic together and transformed it into the purest form of the elements, love.

Which, in her case, came in the form of a perfect little snowflake.

She brought the little love flake close to the barb and they reacted like two magnets of opposite polar forces chasing each other around the table. "This magic is from Hell. But it's not Ereshkigal's."

There were other demons in Hell, but Ereshkigal was their Queen and had dominion over them all. The Dragon Warriors had defeated her and sent her back to its depths. "Who or what else has power like that?"

A group of the Black Dragons all glanced at each other, and the dragon formerly known as Kur-Jara growled. "There are depths of Hell even I haven't ventured into. There could be any number of demons trying to rise to power now that Ereshkigal is trapped in the underworld. But whatever it is, used this spell to mark your mate's soul."

Jett, the Black Dragon Wyvern, scowled, and black smoke rose up from his mouth. "The Black Dragon Brotherhood will assume responsibility for investigating these crimes of Hell. We can't allow anyone to block us from finding our mates."

"But first, we have to find Lena, Jada, and the women here. I won't be going anywhere until we do." If Taika had to move to the mountains of Tennessee and leave the ocean behind for the rest of his days, he would. He'd never stop searching for his mate. He'd only just found her, and he wanted more time with her than one fucking night.

The other Dragon Warriors nodded in agreement, but he could see pity in their eyes. They might have given up hope, but he never would. Ky stood with him, looked around the field and said, "Yes, I do believe Tennessee could make a nice new home for the Blue Dragon Wyr."

The absolute and utter leadership of his King meant everything to him. He sincerely hoped neither he nor Ky would have to fulfill those vows and instead, their mates would simply appear.

Gris, the Gold Wyr Second, snapped to attention, stood up and held his hand up to silence the crowd. Taika recognized when a fellow dragon was speaking to their mate in their head. Gris's mate was Portia, the Queen of the Succubus, and Jada's sister. Perhaps she had some insight to where the girls were being held, or the demon Billy was working with.

Portia did have a slightly unique perspective since she was actually in Hell at the moment, serving as the Winter Shadow. Why hadn't Taika thought of going to her in the first place? "What is she saying, Gris?"

Gris's eyes went wide, he smiled, and pointed to the center of the field. They all turned, and Taika thought his heart was going to explode out of his chest. He heard her voice before he saw her. Coming up from under the ground was some kind of tune about everything being all wrong, but it being all right.

He sprinted to the middle of the field, right alongside Ky. He fully shifted and used his big sharp talons to dig into the ground below them. Had they been right under their feet all along? It couldn't be that easy, could it?

Even as he threw mounds of dirt to the side and between his legs, shadow bubbled up around them. The Black Dragon Warriors surrounded them and bolstered the shadow with their own power over the unearthly element. With a pop and a poof, Portia came careening out of the ground. Gris jumped for her, grabbed her in his arms and immediately shifted, using his great big wings to shield her from the sun.

Right behind her came a very pregnant woman, then Jada. Wait. Where was Lena?

Taika dashed into the shadow and his stomach went haywire. He wasn't made for shadow travel, and it made even the strongest warriors nauseated, but this was something more. There was something malevolent and chaotic in the shadow with him.

"Lena, where are you? Lena, come back to me, love."

No answer.

Wait. Wait. A new song rang through the darkness. "Eye-yee-eye will always love you-ooh-ooh-ooh."

Lena slammed into Taika's chest, knocking them both out of the shadow and into the light of day. Another person came out with her and rolled head over ass several meters across the field. Taika didn't care if that was the First Dragon himself, he had eyes only for Lena.

He shifted back into his human form and grabbed her tight to his chest. "Lena, my Lena. I thought I'd lost you."

"You could never do that, my lovely mate. Jada says

Blue Dragon Warriors are great at finding things that are lost." She was smiling and peppering him with kisses and didn't seem harmed even a little bit.

"Dear Goddess, love. How did you, where have you, aw fuck it, I don't care. I'm so glad to have you back, I could cry a river." That wasn't an exaggeration. If he didn't get himself under control in the next minute or so, this playing field was going to become a pool, or a lake, or maybe even a brand new ocean.

"It's a weird, long story that involves dungeons, and dragons, and demons, and honestly, too much rhubarb for my taste. I promise to tell you every single thing just as soon as I break the eardrums of that pile of poo over there." Lena pointed to the other person and all eyes turned to him.

Billy Whitecap. President of the official Piece of Shit association. "Looks like you're going to have to get in line to exact your revenge, chook."

Mrs. Walker currently had Billy-boy suspended in the air with a noose of fire. He was kicking his feet and screaming, even though her fire was contained and not even burning him.

"Mama? You're... you left the house." Lena stared at her mum and then glanced around the field, doing several double takes at the witches and dragons gathered.

"It was time, baby. I was ready." There was more strength in Mrs. Walker's voice now than ever before.

"Umm. Okay, I'm glad." Lena grabbed Taika's hand and he pulled himself together because she needed his support. She hadn't needed him to rescue her, but she needed him by her side. What a woman. "Maybe don't kill Billy though. I don't think that would be good for your mental health."

The flames in the noose went a bit brighter and Billy's eyes bulged out. "Maybe. Maybe not. We'll see. Won't we, Billy?"

An owl screeched from somewhere in the nearby trees and a darkness rose up out of Billy's chest, made a similar sound, and fled across the field, flying faster than the speed of light. It disappeared and Billy hung limply from the fire noose.

Mrs. Walker lowered his body to the ground. His eyes were open, his chest moved up and down, breathing, but like the catatonic witches from a few days ago, nobody was home. She waved her hand in front of his face and he didn't even blink. "I didn't do that. I swear. Although, he deserved it, whatever it was."

Jett and Neo exchanged glances and Neo shifted into his dragon form and flew off after the mysterious darkness thing.

The Walker witches gathered Billy's body, helped the pregnant woman and Lena's mama into some waiting Utes. Lena waived them off and said a quick goodbye to her mother and promised to check in on her later. Then she rejoined Taika and snuggled up against him.

He wanted only to do one thing, and that was find a cool mountain spring where he could take his mate and show her exactly how much he missed her.

"That was one of our stranger American adventures," Cage said. "I say we finish up these trials, declare a winner, and get back to our homes."

Ky shook his head and growled. "Next year, we're having the games in New Zealand. Weird shit like this doesn't happen on my islands."

Lena looked up at Taika. "Games?"

He pointed up to the sky where the Shifter Games symbols hung in the air. "It's sort of like the Olympics, but apparently with more demons."

"Hey," Ciara suddenly shouted. "Who found the Dragon's egg? I'm dying to know what the perfect gift that manifested for someone's mate was."

Taika chuckled. "It was ice cream. The perfect gift was ice cream."

DRAGON TAILS AND HEAS

"Run, Taika, run. You blue bastard, run." Lena was on her feet whooping and hollering and having the most fun she'd had in pretty much her entire life. Taika was competing in the final heat of the shifter gauntlet, and he was freaking winning.

She raised her hand over her head and shook her fist in circles shouting "whoop, whoop, whoop." A teeny tiny category five tornado circled down from the sky over their heads. For the third time in the last half an hour. Seemed now that her powers were out and proud, they were quite a bit stronger than anyone anticipated.

Fallyn, who was a red fire witch like the Walker family, said that she suspected it was because Lena came from a lengthy line of red witches and was also a Gold Wyr dragon's daughter. There weren't very many mates who had power over more than one element. But it also meant she had a lot of work to do learning how to control it.

Luckily, the King, or, oops, the Wyvern of the Gold Dragons, who was the most powerful controller of the wind and sun elements, snickered at her accidental magic frenzy and made the tornado disappear. "Sorry, Cage, sir. Won't happen again."

Azy, his mate, snorted. "Yes it will. But it's okay. He needs something new to keep him on his toes."

"Oh, yeah. Because our twins aren't enough to do that," Cage grumped, but he gave Lena a wink.

She liked these Dragon Warrior people. Ciara had already invited her to come to Prague to do some wedding planning, Azy said she and Taika could honeymoon at their beach house in Spain, Fallyn suggested they go Christmas ornament shopping together, and Yvaine had really weirdly asked if she and Taika had tried butt stuff yet.

Portia and Jada sat next to Lena, under their big UV blocking shade umbrellas, sun hats, and dark glasses. Jada was laughing at them all. "Welcome to the mates' club. I'll just say, sometimes it's nice to live all the way on the opposite side of the world from the rest of them. Whenever you're ready to come to the Blue Wyr's home, we'll be ready for you. It's nice and calm, and quieter than here."

Lena liked the fun and silly natures of each of the Wyvern mates. But she couldn't discount the fact that she would definitely love to have some quiet time with Taika.

Or you know, noisy, dirty, sexy times, but with some privacy. "I've definitely always wanted to visit New Zealand. I've only ever been to Canada and Mexico, and the rest of you all are so worldly."

"Funny enough, I've never been to either of those two countries. I spent most of my time on the East Coast of the US and a little in Africa and the Middle East where Portia and I are originally from. When were you in Mexico? I've always wanted to learn to make Oaxacan food. I used to watch this show on the Food Network about a woman from there who would go back and visit..." Jada continued on about Mexican food for a whole nother minute.

"Last year in the fall, after the tourist season here." She'd depleted her entire someday jar just on the plane ticket, and then had done some singing for her supper once she got down there. That jar was going in the trash. She didn't need it anymore.

Not just because Taika was a gojillionaire, as were all dragons. Turned out, that hoarding gold and treasures thing was real. But now that she'd talked to her mama and the family about getting some help so she didn't feel stuck here, someday could be anytime she wanted.

"Huh. That's about when we were all in Rogue for the big battle with Hell. No wonder Taika's soul shard didn't go off for you then. I guess he wasn't close enough."

That was interesting. "How close does a soul shard need to be?"

"You know, I don't actually have any idea. Someone

really should write a book about Dragon mating rituals. We could really use a manual or something. Oh look, here they come again." Jada pointed to the five Dragon Warriors, one of each color, zooming out of the trees and toward the finish line.

Taika's dragon took her breath and squeezed it tight, every time she saw him. He was body surfing a magical wave of water across the field. He was neck and neck with a red dragon who was riding in similar style, but on what looked like lava. Crazy.

Lena jumped up again but kept her arms to herself this time. "Gooooo, Tai, gooo."

The finish line was so close, and he put on another burst of water, splashing the front of the lava rider's wave, trying to knock his nearest competitor off balance. The red dragon shot a plume of fire at the water, but it just turned to steam and didn't slow Taika down even a little. Then, at the very last second, a wall of dirt shot up right in front of the two of them, and a Green Dragon Warrior slid down the wall and right onto the awards podium.

The crowd went wild and rushed over to congratulate the winner. Lena pushed her way through them all and over to her beautiful Blue Dragon. His scales sparkled like a million jewels on the water, but none brighter than the soul shard he wore around his neck. *"Sorry you didn't win."*

He snuffled her hair with his snout and replied in her

head. *"It's okay. If I'd won, we'd have to stay for the medal ceremony. Now, I can steal you away and show you the magical lake right here in your mountains."*

Ooh, magic lake was definitely her choice. *"Is it a private lake where we could have loud and boisterous sex? Because that definitely sounds like more fun than a silly medal ceremony."*

Taika opened his talons and motioned for her to crawl into his enormous claw. *"However did you know?"*

He flapped his wings and lifted up into the air. Who would have ever thought she would be flying over the Great Smoky Mountains in the talons of a freaking dragon? They didn't go far before she spotted what looked like some kind of mirage around a tall clump of trees.

Taika headed straight for it and right before it looked like he was going to crash them into the tallest tree of the bunch, the mirage shifted, and a gorgeous lake appeared before them. He swept down right above the water and dragged his other claw through the rippling waves, splashing her with the cool mountain water. *"Welcome to Atagâ'hï."*

Wowee wow. Atagâ'hï was a lake revered in Aniyvwiya indigenous folk tales that only animals seeking refuge could find. Of course a powerful water dragon would be able to access it. As they approached the banks, he shifted in mid-flight, wrapped her into his arms and said, "Take a deep breath, we're going in."

Lena filled her lungs with air and closed her eyes, dropping her head to his chest. They splashed down into the water and the lush silence of being surrounded by the lake overtook all of her senses. Ripples went out around them, and she could see everything as clear as day. *"Tai, this is amazing."*

He swirled the water around them so gently, it was like they were dancing. He brushed his lips across hers and then along her jaw, back to her ear, and down to the spot on her neck where the sparkling blue symbol of his dragon's mark decorated her skin like the best kind of tattoo. The kind that reflected what was in her heart.

She used her own power of the wind to keep the air in her mouth and lungs fresh so she could stay under the water with him longer than humanly possible. But sooner than she expected, Taika propelled them toward the shore and into a surprisingly warm pool against one of the banks.

Lena concentrated, flicked her wrist, and sent their soaked clothes flying and draped them over some nearby bushes. The weather was more than perfect in this magical place, their clothes would dry quickly and smell of sunshine when they were ready to get dressed again. Which, she hoped, wouldn't be for an awfully long time.

"I knew you would be gorgeous all wet." Taika bent his head to the crook of her neck and lapped at the water droplets on her skin.

"Oh, I'm wet all right." She groaned and pushed her

fingers into his hair to hold his mouth to her skin and over her dragon's mark a little longer. Her heart picked up the pace and skipped a few beats just for fun.

"You're wet here." He bent his head and licked down one of her breasts bobbing in the water, finding her nipple and giving it some much needed attention. "And here." He moved to her other breast and tugged at that nipple with his teeth, sending lovely shockwaves of desire through her body.

Taika slid his hands down her sides, tracing her curves all the way to her wide hips. Then he tugged her against him, pressing his erection against her belly. "But where else are you wet? I'd better check every square centimeter of you."

Taika ducked under the water and Lena got to find out exactly how creative a Blue Dragon Warrior could be with his tongue... and his tail. He laid her back in the water, so she floated with her arms out at her sides, balancing her. Then he spread her legs and buried his face in between them.

"More, Taika. I need more of you." Floating like this, she couldn't reach for his head and guide him to where she wanted him, so she tried using their mental connection to show him what she wanted.

Taika had ideas all his own. *"You're a dirty girl. Let's see if I can make you even dirtier."*

He shifted just his tail, and it slipped through the water, tickling first her toes, then fondling its way up her thighs, snuck underneath and swirled around her butt, the tip teasing her with little caresses over the tight rose of her anus. Lena's belly tingled and her mind went haywire with ideas of just exactly how dirty he was talking about.

"I see you're already absolutely filthy and we'll be fulfilling several of those fantasies soon enough." Taika pushed some of his own very imaginative scenarios about what he'd like to do to her with his tail into her mind. Those images pushed her right over the edge into a searing climax. She moaned out so loud, it sent a whole flock of birds flying away.

Taika didn't give her even a minute to float in that bliss before he positioned his tail into a barrier behind her that he pushed her up against. He kissed her hard, pushing his tongue in and out of her mouth, while thrusting his hips against hers, matching the rhythm. She could taste her own essence on him and that did nothing to cool the lust raging inside of her for him. Always for him.

He broke the kiss and nibbled his way down to her mark, pressing softer kisses over the dragon's mark. "I will never get enough of the taste of you coming on my tongue, sweet Lena."

"I haven't even gotten to taste you yet."

"Fuck, Lena. I'd love to see your lips around my cock, but there's something I want even more first."

Taika gave her another searing kiss and then took one step back. He slipped the necklace that had his soul shard on it off of his neck and looked down at it. "Lena, my love. I was worried that I was broken and might never find you. I think perhaps the First Dragon and the White Witch wanted me to more fully appreciate the gift they were giving me when they helped me find you."

Aww, that was so incredibly tender. "Is it mean of me to say I'm glad they did? I wouldn't want our love story any other way."

"Naughty witch. But you're right. This is exactly as it was supposed to be. Fate did not steer us wrong." Taika grinned and slipped the necklace over Lena's head.

The moment it hit her skin, the magic between them exploded, filling the sky with not only the blue light of his soul, the golden music of hers, but with the absolute feeling of true love.

"I claim you as my mate, Lena, and ask that you take this piece of my soul as your own to keep and safeguard." He pressed his hand over the shard on her chest, and Lena put hers on top of his.

"I am yours, and you are mine, Taika. My dragon, my love. If I could, I'd give you a piece of my soul too." She paused for a moment and listened to something the wind whispered to her. "Ah, but perhaps I don't need to, because my soul already is yours, and will be forever."

"Forever." Taika pulled her into his arms, and they showed each other just what forever meant, with their mouths, with their bodies, and with their love. He lifted her legs, wrapping her knees around him, and notched his cock at her entrance.

"This time I want to see you come. I want your eyes locked with mine so I can see in your eyes what each and every thrust of my cock into your hot cunt does to you." He pushed in nice and slow, driving her mad as she felt each inch of him spreading her open, grazing along all the most sensitive places inside. She whimpered with the pleasure of it until he was fully seated, and she felt like they were one once again.

Lena closed her eyes and tipped her face to the sun, breathing in the pleasure in deep, long breaths. But the very tip of Taika's tail wrapped around her throat and forced her face back down. Her body clenched hard around his, and she let out a garbled moan.

"Ah, you like that do you, chook? I told you I wanted your eyes on mine." He pressed her harder into the thick stalk of the part of his tail she was sitting on, and then began his torturously slow thrusts. But even he could only take so much and before she even had to beg, he sped up until he was pounding into her, sending them both into a frenzy of passion.

His tail curled tighter around her neck, and the tip wound down between her breasts, all the way between the two of them, and he pushed it between her legs. With each thrust, his tail flickered across clit, almost like his tongue, and Lena couldn't hold on any longer.

She grabbed his face so she could fulfill his wish of looking into each other's eyes as they came together. His flashed with the deep blue of his dragon rising up inside of him. His beast's eyes stared back at her and he growled and thrust into her hard this time, his cock jerking with his own release. "Mine. My mate. Mine."

Lena's own magic lit inside of her, matching his, and she claimed him too as she joined him in the most intense and satisfying orgasm. "I'm yours. Forever yours, my Dragon."

They made love in the warm pool until the sun began to set. She didn't mind the cool air because it meant she got to snuggle up with him. They talked long into the night about their future together, the possibility of children, where they would live, and how she could hone her powers to help in the Dragons' continued battles to fight evil in all its forms.

Just like in Dolly's song, Lena had felt like she was barely getting by. Until she opened her heart not just to Taika, but to who she really was too, and that was the truest happily ever after she could ever have.

GRAB the final book in the Dragons Love Curves series to read next — Merry Me

WANT a little bit more Lena and Taika? Join my Curvy Connection Newsletter and get a bonus chapter!

. . .

NEED to know more about the mysterious darkness? Neo, the Black Dragon Second Wyvern and his mate Kady are the first up in the Black Dragon Brotherhood series where we'll fight the darkness and find true love!

Grabbed their story in Tamed.

ACKNOWLEDGMENTS

Big thanks to my proofreader, Chrisandra. She probably hates commas as much as I do now. All the remaining errors are all my fault. I'm sure I screwed it up somewhere.

I'm ever grateful to my writer pals for helping my finish another book and not thinking I'm as crazy as I think I am.

I am so very grateful to have readers who will join my on my crazy book adventures where there will ALWAYS be curvy girls getting happy ever afters!

Without all of you, I wouldn't be able to feed my cats (or live the dream of a creative life!)

Thank you so much to all my Patreon Book Dragons!

An enormous thanks to my Official Biggest Fans Ever. You're the best book dragons a curvy girl author could ask for~

Thank you so much for all your undying devotion for me and the characters I write. You keep me writing (almost) every day.

Hugs and Kisses and Signed Books and Swag for you from me! I am so incredibly grateful for each of you and am awed by your support.

- Helena E.
- Alida H.
- Daphine G.
- Bridget M.
- Stephanie F.
- Danielle T.
- Marea H.
- Marilyn C.
- Mari G.
- Jessica W.

Shout out to my Official VIP Fans!
Extra Hugs and signed books to you ~

- Jeanette M.
- Kerrie M.
- Michele C.
- Corinne A.
- Deborah S.
- Frania G.
- Jennifer B.
- Elizabeth R.

ALSO BY AIDY AWARD

Dragons Love Curves

Chase Me

Tease Me

Unmask Me

Bite Me

Cage Me

Baby Me

Defy Me

Surprise Me

Dirty Dragon

Crave Me

Dragon Love Letters - Curvy Connection Exclusive

Slay Me

Play Me

Merry Me

The Black Dragon Brotherhood

Tamed

Tangled

Twisted

Fated For Curves

A Touch of Fate

A Tangled Fate

A Twist of Fate

Alpha Wolves Want Curves

Dirty Wolf

Naughty Wolf

Kinky Wolf

Hungry Wolf

Grumpy Wolves

Filthy Wolf

The Fate of the Wolf Guard

Unclaimed

Untamed

Undone

Undefeated

Claimed by the Seven Realms

Protected

Stolen

Crowned

By Aidy Award and Piper Fox

Big Wolf on Campus

Cocky Jock Wolf

Bad Boy Wolf

Heart Throb Wolf

Hot Shot Wolf

Contemporary Romances by Aidy Award

The Curvy Love Series

Curvy Diversion

Curvy Temptation

Curvy Persuasion

The Curvy Seduction Saga

Rebound

Rebellion

Reignite

Rejoice

Revel

ABOUT THE AUTHOR

Aidy Award is a curvy girl who kind of has a thing for stormtroopers. She's also the author of the popular Curvy Love series and the hot new Dragons Love Curves series.

She writes curvy girl erotic romance, about real love, and dirty fun, with happy ever afters because every woman deserves great sex and even better romance, no matter her size, shape, or what the scale says.

Read the delicious tales of hot heroes and curvy heroines come to life under the covers and between the pages of Aidy's books. Then let her know because she really does want to hear from her readers.

Connect with Aidy on her website. www.AidyAward.com get her Curvy Connection, and join her Facebook Group - Aidy's Amazeballs.

Printed in Great Britain
by Amazon